CROWD CRUSH

Crowd Crush

A NOVEL

Carlos José Camblor

First paperback edition March 2022

Book design by Stewart A. Williams

Cover photo by Amir Arabshahi @ Unsplash

ISBN 978-0-578-36412-4

Rocinante Press

www.cjcamblor.com

Acknowledgements

Special thanks to LeAnne Howe, Vineet Date, Duncan Murrell, Kankana Basu, and Stewart Williams.

For Joan.

Les événements les plus douteux sont certainement ceux qui ont été observés par le plus grand nombre de personnes.

—Gustave Le Bon, *Psychologie des Foules*

SEATAC/ATL

blog structure   buffering

compartmentalization   compression

digital identity   enhanced reality

glitched reality   prognostication

Stone Mountain   Theater of Memory

Light blue, green, dark blue in a triple wave down the side of the train. Mount Baker, Columbia City, Othello, Rainier Beach, Tukwila, the airport. Seattle's newish light rail, the Link, is the jumping-off place, where the journey begins, the first place I can stop to start my blog. Because of the way blogs work, the way posts stack up with each new one on top of the one before it, this entry at the beginning of the trip is destined to be on the bottom at the finish. The middle will remain the middle, but the end will become the beginning.

Ever since their arrival, I've had problems with the reverse structure of their format. If they haven't already been following the blog, people might read the posts backward through time, which destroys any possibility of a plot parabola—you would have to have resolutions on either side. Stories happen chronologically, in forward mode, even if the parts get retold out of order, so how can a blog be a good read if its time scheme is inverted? Stitched into its configuration is the way reality piles up, which usually—sometimes hopefully—lacks any kind of intrinsic story arc.

But I'm doing it anyway. Welcome and farewell.

I got the grant to go to Germany and India for my research, and after I visit my family in Atlanta for a few days, I'm headed to Spain to do some climbing with Brad from Boulder, and to visit my father in Asturias. After that, I get down to work looking into the 2010 Love Parade catastrophe in Duisburg, and finally I'll be studying the crowd crush event that happened at the 2008 Navratri festival in Jodhpur.

My therapist recommended that I keep a journal of my trip to help me deal with my problems, and I figure I might as well post it online. I'm only a few paragraphs in, and it's already allowed me to hide from everyone on the train for a few minutes. But I guess that's not what I'm supposed to use it for.

After Rainier Beach, the train makes a leap into open space, leaving the ground and going elevated for a stretch, a prelude to the airplane's jump a few hours away, and I told myself to think to myself that I love her. I couldn't remember the last time I left the surface.

Scroll down.

I'm writing this beneath the massive, concave, glass grid of the atrium between concourses, where a quiet rumble regularly announces another liftoff. With real life being compared more and more to digital media, it's easy to imagine I'm watching an enormous video installation over the food court, with airplanes taking off and landing in an endless loop above the Starbucks island. Almost everyone ignores it.

Not many phone booths anymore—it's all in the ether now. What used to be a primary feature of airport architecture has been replaced by vending machines and sales booths, or not replaced by anything yet. Stretches of wall space with rows of jacks, but no phones, wait to catch up with what comes next.

Security wasn't as bad as I expected, but the line for self check-in freaked me out a little. The tranquilizers I took on top of my usual meds made everything fuzzy but tolerable. I did my counting.

Coming inside from the light rail, I saw an old man fall down while mounting the up escalator—a small public emergency which I watched unfold but steered clear of—and during the body scan I remembered what my doctor said about all the wasted information. He proposed you should be able to sign a form to have the body scan data sent to your physician or radiologist for interpretation. Instead first they dumb it down, then they delete it. I joked that it sounded like my love life, dumbed down and deleted, but it didn't really make sense. He looked at me funny. You would think that doctors would be trained not to look at you funny.

I made my way to the end of the concourse, sliding past the long, trippy Rube Goldberg music box installed next to the moving sidewalk, and I found the windows above my gate at the end of the terminal had been painted into a fake, stained glass mosaic of the zodiac, adding a churchy feeling that I thought was appropriate. In the short list of places where atheists think about God, airports sit comfortably near the top.

After walking back here to the Starbucks, I said fuck it and paid to hook up to the airport's Wi-Fi. I checked my email, and the weather on my flight path, then I was overwhelmed by possibilities again. Without something specific to search for, I sat here and stared at the browser screen. There's got to be a word for the quiet terror of all the options. The Greek for "infinite webs" with another -*phobia* tacked on the end? What good is it all if you can't remember or decide what to look for?

The whole thing is just a construction of memory anyway, a massive compartmentalization of details stored in smaller and smaller boxes, so I'm not surprised that my largest issues with the World Wide Web are essentially reflexive. The internet's existence, albeit an electronic one, means there's no need for mnemonic devices anymore. We need less and less memory in our brains as we fill up our machines with it. Exactly what we require is what we let fall from our grasp, because it's already everywhere around us, except that we don't really let go of it. The world has never before seen so many people clutching handheld electronic devices, and here at the airport the phenomenon is at its apex. I hid from it all in my own little machine. I could have studied more crowd crush videos, but I told myself to try to just be on vacation until I get to Germany.

We like to think of the web as weightless and invisible, but I
read statistics about its growing corporeality the other day.
An estimated 1.5 percent of the world's energy is being used
now to run the server farms and data centers that contain
the so-called cloud, and scientists disagree about the average
carbon dioxide emissions from a single search engine inquiry—depending on who you ask, it's anywhere from 0.2 to 7
grams per click. But what I find most amazing is that all of
this energy and infrastructure is used to corral a network of
streaming electrons that, when added up theoretically, have a
mass of around 0.00004 ounces per year. That's 1.5 percent
of the world's energy used to transport and corral something
that's next to nothing.

It wasn't very far from papyrus to pixels, from scrolls to scroll-
ing, and now here we are living life at 0.72 megabytes per
second. Just like with text on paper, there's way more blank
on the so-called page than black. Emblematic of the web's
high-speed vacuousness, an empty message box popped up on
my screen and asked me to okay it, but okay what? There was
nothing to okay. I played it safe and rebooted the browser.

Because of the way it's expanding through a sort of anti-space, unseen, I prefer to imagine it as a hive instead of a
web. It's like something dark that maintains walls and limits
inside cracks and attics, a darkness growing within a darkness,
but it defines itself more by where it doesn't exist than by
where it does. Like with social insects, the communication
within habitations is chemical, almost instantaneous, but
outside their insular structure the world goes on, unnoticing,
uninformed, unburdened. Isn't it ultimately a place to hide

everything and to hide from everything, where we're all in it together and it all makes sense? Everything inside the hive is interspecies action and communication. It is us in a way the outside is not.

And inside the hive if it's not reflexive odds are it's redundant. Now the news is the news, what's on Wikipedia is what they're talking about on NPR, and some of the edits of the web encyclopedias become items on their own news pages. Whether or not a particular video is available on sharing sites might be a hot topic on Morning Edition, making it all seem like a growing feedback loop of information about information about information. Experts in the rapidly expanding field of internetology have likened the whole thing to blind and naked mole rats squeaking inside echoing Habitrails, and my favorite parts of this transmedia, augmented, and accelerated reality have got to be the new interactive advertisements. I'm so happy I can follow my corn chips or my yogurt on social networking sites and see where my banana was cloned.

I wonder what Don Giulio Camillo—the sixteenth century inventor of the Theater of Memory, a primitive precursor to the world's digital data storage systems—would think of the saturation of pointless details being filed away in his upgraded collection of classified cabinets. Would he compare it to a flood or a mold consuming his playhouse?

How appropriate that Camillo chose to call his memory construction a theater, the same word military strategists use now for the online battlefield. Just the other day they said in the media that Israel has got a new Internet Fighting Team, and that other mildly more authoritarian countries like Estonia are considering drafting cyber defense armies from the ranks of their most electronically talented teenagers.

Since I mentioned Israel, I might as well go ahead and mention Nazis in the blog. I read about Godwin's Law the other day: It states that as an internet forum grows in length the odds that Hitler or Nazis will get mentioned approaches one hundred percent. There. Got that out of the way. The pressure is off.

I snickered at my laptop and the guy two seats down laughed at his Blackberry, a sort of gestural interfacing that ac-knowledged our likeness, but with a signal far below the high bandwidth of face to face. With a quick scan of the crowd I saw more than half the people were engaged with a phone, or a PDA, or a player of some sort, and having seen more and more old men looking lost inside their devices in public, it seemed to me there must be some kind of eventual recon-nection between the baby talk of modern electronics—*my myspace, if you youtube, google my ipod, my facespace, mybook, wikigoogletube*—and the childlike wasteland of our approaching senilities.

Scroll down.

Reprise. As we left the ground, I thought to myself that I love her.

In the absence of any kind of god, thinking about loving somebody takes its place. But I'm such an ass. I didn't think about my mother, or the other family and friends who actually deserve my love, but a self-proclaimed tart who isn't sure she loves me back. Who I can talk about like this because I'm fairly certain she won't bother reading this anytime soon. I guess you're not supposed to go there in a blog. There's the so-called internal voice, and then there's the so-called external voice. In any case, she'll agree, now or later, that I'm an ass.

I was in a window seat, and we climbed over extended parking lots, and the chrome and mirrors in the rows of cars released jewel flashes like light on waves. Mt. Rainier—sitting magnificent, having nothing to do with the British rear admiral from whom it received its moniker—was more impressive from the air than anything that should ever be named after a man, especially a guy who fought against the US in the Revolutionary War. We climbed higher, *Up-Arrow, Up-Arrow, Up-Arrow*, and then we were surrounded by the screensaver of clouds.

When I used to live in the San Juan Islands, I kept a hitch-hiking diary in which I tried to sum up in one line the various drivers and their cars. I attempted to do the same with the guy sitting next to me, except I could leave out the description of the car: skinny gray-haired outdoor enthusiast with an annoyingly deep voice wearing five-toed sports sandals. Next seat down, making chitchat with him about his footwear: heavyset Southern Baptist or Methodist woman with overt cross necklace and swollen ankles.

The shuffle program picked up my music exactly where I left it before I went to sleep last night, and it was sort of like those twelve hours of in-between never existed. I couldn't help thinking about the missing parts and the buffering, the start

and stop of modern monitors, the glitched, or chopped, or
stalled of the webcam world.

Now everything stutters like Max Headroom, and though the
New Coke spokesperson is mostly forgotten, he's never seemed
so far ahead of his time. Nothing works like it used to. The
screens get smaller and smaller, the audio doesn't match the
video, and it jumps and flickers forward through time. Phone
calls were generally crystal clear when I was a child, and you
could hear what the other person was saying at the same time
you were talking. Now, despite—or I guess because of—our
advancements and mobility, I can't understand much of what's
delivered or not delivered over the wireless network. It's been
said before, we're forced to recover from the improvements.

More tranquilizers. Little baby blue ones with the number
555 imprinted on one side. Now that I was scheduled to be
stationary I could risk further sedation.

Looking out the window, down on the clouds reminded
me how I've been watching the sunrise lately via satellite
stop-motion on the weather web page. A black sea becomes
white clouds as the rolling, looping image gradually demonstrates dawn, making me feel like I'm actually awake and witnessing it. Online I can see the sunrise better than anywhere
in my neighborhood.

Now the images are so crisp, the definition so clean, that the
virtual or reproduced often transcends the real. The videos
and photos on the website might present the music festival,
or the club, or the art opening as cooler than it really was, or

will be, and if you've actually been there it's strange to see it online later, and then to wish it had been as vivid as the reproduction. Enhancing the past seems like a mix-up of verb tenses, but I guess it will have been nothing new.

The screens are holes not windows. We're all peering into holes like the magic, movable black circles of cartoons that anything can go into or come out of. It's the keyhole phenomenon, where what you see beyond the tiny opening is much larger than the opening. And if you look closely, all the holes on the screen cast shadows on one another, depending on which is on top, and if you get a drop of moisture on the monitor it will magnify the red, blue, and green pixels inside itself. The letter games I enjoyed in my youth—creating words out of the random vertical alignment of letters in horizontal text—are gone on the computer screen, where *Control Plus* or *Control Minus* instantly rearranges the formatting of the paragraph. The hidden words, the steganographies, disappear, losing in the process any supposed significance. The whole screen might shift or slide suddenly while you're reading it, as it shrinks or expands or reformats itself, and as we pack more and more images onto the surface it's increasingly like hieroglyphics and story murals and less and less like twenty-six letters repeating in a long line that's chopped up and organized in rows on sequential pages. The bell is ringing. Let us sing another of Paper's eulogies.

I'm increasingly preoccupied with the lost in-betweens, as everything gets digitally compressed or cut. I tried to explain to my girlfriend Lydia how they can create smaller, simplified music files by removing redundant information, and she said

it was like fluorescent light-bulbs, which appear to be on all
the time but are actually flashing at a rate that's faster than
the eye can see. She said she couldn't stand living in a strobing
world, whether or not she could see it strobing. This flight is
one of the lost in-betweens too. I go down a long, strange hallway, and take a seat, they close the doors, and I stare through
a screen or look through a window for a few hours, then they
open the doors later and I walk out another hallway and I'm
somewhere else. Where did the in-between go? And why is the
screen analogy usually windows instead of doors? Why isn't it
Microsoft Doors? Is it because you don't usually go through
windows, but you go through doors. Unless you just stare at
them. And aren't doors and windows really just types of holes?

I could really feel the tranquilizer at this point, which was
kind of like not feeling I guess. Perhaps I would dream of the
pie charts and Pac-Men, or the megapixels of green and tan
circles and triangles and squares that are the farms of Kansas
from thirty-six thousand feet.

Buffering, please wait.

Orange, yellow-orange, and blue, in three straight stripes
down the side of the train. After leaving Hartsfield-Jackson
on MARTA, it was College Park, Eastpoint, Lakewood,
Oakland City, West End—parts of the South that might as
well be Timbuktu to me, even though I grew up here.

When we were children in the mostly-white suburbs of
North Atlanta in the '80s, our elders and educators were
little interested in integrating us with the African American

populations of Atlanta so nearby. We were never taken to the King Memorial, or Ebenezer Baptist, but to the Coca-Cola Museum, and Stone Mountain, where the largest bas-relief sculpture in the world proudly displays a tribute to the Confederacy's generals, blasted onto the side of the biggest dome of exposed granite east of the Mississippi in an artistic feat comparable to Mt. Rushmore's, but thankfully less iconic in the nation's consciousness. They didn't tell me on our day trips there that the Ku Klux Klan was brought back to life in a secret cross-burning ceremony on top of Stone Mountain during the night after Thanksgiving in 1915, and that the Klan was largely responsible for the commissioning of the "artwork." While this was stunning to learn as an adult living in Seattle, the part I find most amazing is that with the white population of the Atlanta area becoming increasingly obese and sedentary, to walk the 1.3 miles up the mountain today is to have one of the most culturally diverse pilgrimages available in America. It looks like all Sikhs and Columbians, Slovaks and Vietnamese on the hill, not white supremacists.

Now that I'm older it's my own fault that I don't know these southern neighborhoods, that I haven't explored them during my infrequent visits home. Everyone else on the train knew exactly what type of guy I was—I was the white guy who only uses MARTA to go from the airport to the North End.

Garnett, Five Points, Peachtree Center, Civic Center. I hadn't gotten off at one of these stops in years, since Emory University Hospital was still called Crawford Long, when my high school friends and I would salute the man who helped popularize the anesthetic diethyl ether—one of our favorite

recreational inhalants—as the intercom said his name while
approaching North Avenue.

Crawford is remembered for removing a tumor from the neck
of one James A. Venable in 1842, with the help of ether's
palliative effects. Members of this same Venable family owned
Stone Mountain from the 1880s right into the 1950s. Samuel
Venable gave permission for the Klan to use his family's mountain, and stood with them during the group's first ceremony
that night in 1915, and I'm not sure what kind of connection
I'm trying to make here, but it seems like part of something.

Irrational things don't fit into the algorithm. Perhaps I'm making nothing out of something again, but the coincidental and
the serendipitous get flagged when run through the equation.
Sometimes that's what the set of functions is designed to find.
More often it's the mundane that's of interest to the mar-
keter's math models—your shopping patterns, average online
expenditure, the nebulous demographic estimate of your consumption—but the mind's own research trajectories are more
difficult to understand. No computer was counting how many
times the guy across from me tapped his toe, but I couldn't
stop myself from doing the addition. And when the total was
eighteen—the same number of stops until I had to get off at
North Springs—what was I to make of it? My therapist said it
was okay to count things, but he didn't have anything to say
about what the numbers mean when they line up just so.

*Midtown, Art Center, Lindbergh Center, Buckhead, Medical
Center.* It's hard not to think everything is predicted by the
bigger equation, but my other self—the avatar made up of

the zeros and ones that summarize my commercial and web activities, a life as determined by debit transactions and mouse clicks—has no idea what he's being used for, and has no idea how his actions might affect the future or be anticipated in the present. With more than a small percentage of online inquiries being self-searches—people looking for themselves or at their homes from above—the data has assembled a recursive ghost, which, thinking about thinking about myself, seems completely appropriate.

Ghosts and goblins are more real than they've ever been. Digital representations of people live long after their physical forms are burned or buried, and their accounts continue to be administered by digital angels, creating unprecedented legal issues concerning the rights of a simulacrum, and the rights of the fans, friends, or families to protect, change, or delete the phantom of their departed beloved.

Indeed, we're living in a world where our struggles are more and more often about user authentication than sustenance or safety—more and more about how to log into a particular ethereal domain and less and less about any corporeal particulars.

They're talking about a new system of user authentication called EPIC, the Evolved Personalized Information Construct, a system of algorithmic character analysis that knows who you are better than you do, and is capable of foolproofing the analysis of identity by cataloging everything from your online masturbation frequency and duration, to your preferences for liberal or conservative news outlets. They've promised to remove today's identity struggles by providing electronic passports, touchless consent, anonymizers, and fraud protec-tion code. Lie detection software has even been invented that reads text for inconsistencies and problems with voice, and I can't help but wonder what would happen if you fed the prose polygraph machine pure fiction.

Other new software was invented that determined April 11, 1954 was the least eventful day in recorded history, and I wonder what's coming next from the algorithms and the ag-gregators. What unexpected insights into life are coming from the machinations of the growing goddess Memory and her ever evolving, molting, multiplying gate-keepers?

Dunwoody, Sandy Springs. The city gave way to suburbia, and as I read the signs speeding by I knew there were no arbors at The Arbors Apartments, or blue herons at Blue Heron Golf Club, but there was a high gate around Highgate Towne Homes.

I will dumb myself down to fit in during my short stay here, like the lowest common denominator of my self. I will slow down my speech pattern and begin to draw out "y'all" unconsciously.

North Springs. The stop is essentially a large parking garage. Where else but in Atlanta does the subway exit leave you in such limbo? Nothing but empty cars and concrete. No bath-rooms, no bodegas. Nothing for you if you walk out to the road either. Nowhere to eat or get a cup of coffee, only office buildings and more parking lots.

My mom showed up late because she's scared to sit in her car and wait for me here alone, and I don't blame her. Even with, or maybe because of, all the surveillance cameras, the place is disconcerting, although at least it was crowded with cars instead of people.

We plug in more and more cameras in order to take video of more and more nothing, and now they've got continuous, closed-circuit home monitoring for geriatrics—countless Alzheimer's reality shows coming for all of us—devices that, combined with GPS tracking, are capable of knowing whether you've fallen down, or stopped moving, or haven't been to the bathroom, and then notifying your selected responder as necessary. In a few years, they will be selling this to me for my mother.

As caring for humans becomes virtual, and machines are incorporated into the execution of our life functions, it seems perfectly normal that technology adopts the language of our biology in return. As technology is mostly about things for sale, "ecosystem" is now used interchangeably with "market," and "lifecycle" is mostly a business term. Languages and lingos are cross-pollinating in a myriad of ridiculous ways as light-speed communications mix with the hieroglyphs of screen commands and the cybergenetics of memory. An Icelandic artist had the text of one of his poems encrypted into the genetic sequence of a supposedly harmless bacterium, and then he released it into nature to replicate infinitely. He hopes the hearty little bug will survive the eventual destruction of our planet and float through space for eons before germinating in a distant, remote unknown.

I'm forced to wonder if he really thinks his poem is that good.

There's occasional talk at school about The Singularity, when the machines will become alive, something akin to the inverse of our current dynamic of becoming machines. There's even an organization set up to protect us against it, The Singularity Institute— thousands of geeks networking about the liminal line that defines consciousness. Myself, I seriously doubt the networks will ever come alive because we'll never let them. People like to control things. Conversely, maybe that's exactly why we'll keep trying.

According to some of my IT friends at the lab, what is coming, whether or not you think the systems are sentient, is an increasing ability to see into the future, and while you might immediately want to argue about where forecasting starts and prognostication ends, I can't help but remind the reader that the future has always been heretical. At least until recently.

It started with small things like web calendars for future events, and radio playlists recorded for later that became available early. But as correlator tools like Google Trends continue to evolve, and as the data they crunch includes an increasingly large amount of information about the future, the programs are forced either to buffer the present to hold back what lies ahead, or to simply allow the future into their algorithms and let it exist with us contemporaneously. They didn't think it was possible, but now that they've let the programs run with it, they're seeing what will come with as much accuracy as what came, and it's the present that's become increasingly indeterminate to their machines.

I'm not sure it makes me feel any better knowing that the math proves what-must-be is the same as what-was, and that it's the what-is that is most unlike the other two. It's reassuring in some ways. It's just what I suspected on some level. In other ways it seems to be contributing to an increasingly unhinged condition, because our *now* ends up being a state of continuously buffering the rest of the world.

Sending.

BARCELONA

September 12, 2011

airport anxiety   appropriate audience

castells   crowd safety

emergence   herd behavior

human stampede   social anxiety disorder

spontaneous order   stampede prevention

Scroll back up before we get to El Prat.

The flight out of Hartsfield-Jackson wasn't as easy as the one out of SeaTac. It was early in the morning and there were no empty bathroom stalls, so I was forced to vomit into the trashcan in front of a bunch of men waiting in line to crap.

There's a special species of tears shed during regurgitation, when the muscles in your abdomen won't stop seizing, and it's hard to breathe. Friday morning in that overcrowded shit-den, where I was only intermittently able to inhale, the fecal air was putrid enough to induce more than the usual amount of painful gut convulsions before I was able to regain my concept of composure, wash my face off, and exit. Those guys in line were uncomfortable witnesses to that embarrassing breed of weeping.

I guess all in all it wasn't a full-on panic attack, but a bout of nausea nonetheless. The extra tranquilizers did their job to a point but failed to deal with my stomach, and public puking is perhaps the most humiliating sort. When you're already aware that you're having an episode because of your fear of humiliation in the first place, well...

Writing about it a few days later is different though. You can be sort of proud of your suffering when it's part of a larger story. Then again, there is no larger story. This is only a blog post.

Since I'm on this journey to do crowd crush research in Germany and India, I can't help but think the Atlanta airport deserves my amateur crowd safety analysis. With a quarter of a million passengers moving through each day, it's the busiest airport in the US, and the possibilities of crowd events precipitating from various commonplace and inevitable emergencies are very real and pertinent.

They built the place big, planning ahead for ATL to be a transportation hub—a model that had been proven by the railroads in the city's past—and while it always feels crowded now, my cousin Carl remembers running through the miles of massive empty halls when he was a child. He told me about how during Christmas of 1980, when the airport had just opened, he was stuck there with my aunt and my other cousins when their flight kept getting delayed during a winter storm. He said he's never experienced anything like it again in his life, the multitude of moving sidewalks, and automated subways, and endless escalators, and all of it brand new and working perfectly for next to nobody. It was like the world's biggest, heated playground just for him and his siblings.

Now look at it.

Try to find a place to be alone.

At ATL, I prefer to walk the underground hallways between terminals instead of riding the packed trains. These long, pedestrian passages are some of the quietest places in the airport. On this trip, I noticed the emergency exit doors near the subways are equipped with timers so the doors don't open immediately. As someone who's been researching ingress and egress necessities for large crowds, I've learned this sort of false alarm prevention device can end up having lethal trade-offs. There's usually some compromise between safety and convenience.

It was the tenth anniversary of 9/11, and the news on the screens in the terminal kept recycling the footage of planes crashing into towers, and the towers crashing down.

On the flight, I had an empty seat on one side, and a little old lady from Saragossa on the other. She was just like an abuelita in an Almodóvar film, almost a caricature, with the high voice, the rosary beads, and the swollen ankles above her pumps. I moved over one seat to give us both some space, so our conversation was limited. I swallowed some sleeping pills after the first beverage cart and then slept through most of what I believe to have been an uneventful flight.

Okay, scroll back to Barcelona.

Still in a bit of a fog when I took the RENFE train from El Prat, the chemicals wore off after I made the transfer to the metro at the Passeig de Gràcia station, and the ride became difficult to deal with while I headed for the *hostal*.

Instead of looking at people, I stared at the subway map. There is a definite V-ness to the city's metro diagram, with the lines appearing to come down at forty-five degree angles, and there's a little "v" accenting the larger one at the Diagonal station. The TMB logo is the three red capitals inside a white, olive-shaped spot. A shadow/tail thing on the left side suggests movement, making it resemble a quotation mark or comma. It is usually presented on a red field. Municipal logos in Spain generally involve red.

Right now, on this screen, I'm writing at Ambar, a café in the El Raval barrio, just southwest of La Rambla, within the narrow streets of Old Town, also called Chinatown, not far from Fernando Botero's famous cat sculpture. I'm staying nearby at the Hostal Gat Chino, which I'm assuming is named after the sculpture and the neighborhood, but I have yet to confirm it.

The coffees keep adding up, attempting to reach an equilibrium with the tranquilizers. If I don't look up from the screen I can feel normal.

But I'm getting ahead of myself. If you accept that the past is at the top and future at the bottom, then it's *Up-Arrow* again until we get to the now.

I checked in at the hostal and locked up my luggage before going to meet up with my old friend Angela. She moved to Barcelona after college and married a Spaniard, and she's been totally happy here. I can't help but admit that seeing her and remembering the good times we had together touches me with a sense of personal disappointment because I haven't done things as exciting with my own life. But perhaps this is a case of inappropriate audience. You don't talk about those things in a travel blog.

She took me to an expat party in the Gràcia barrio, with lots of beautiful people and cava, and I forget everyone's names but remember feeling not quite capable conversationally. I was mostly in my head, thinking about another time in my life, before the fears showed up; thinking about Angela on a summer night in Portland, under the bushes in the park, or holding hands shoe-skating down frozen sidewalks in December.

We were married at the 24 Hour Church of Elvis once when I visited her, and while I'm sure she married others there, it remains the only time I've ever wed, whether or not it was real. I lost the plastic ring that was dispensed during the coin-op ceremony, but I still have the memory of the ice storm, and her purple rubber boots, and driving to the drugstore to buy condoms. They were closed, and we went ahead and fucked in the car in the parking lot. But later she kept getting cooler and I went the other way. Is this what I'm supposed to write about?

Angela and I passed clubs on the way back after the party, and she thought maybe we should go in and dance, and I couldn't bring myself to tell her that the thought terrified me.

I mentioned my jetlag, and reminded her that she worked in the morning. I said it looked like it was about to rain. I steered clear of the fear and walked her home. I guess by blogging about it I'm telling her now.

The thunder and lightning arrived as we got back to her place in Eixample, and we went up to the roof with umbrellas to watch the sky explode with light. There were taller buildings around us, so it didn't seem completely insane, but I did suggest we weren't being very smart. She dragged on a ciga-rette and said lightning didn't seem like such a bad way to go overall, then linked her elbow with mine to resume watching for the brilliant electric world-rips over the old city.

It was impressive. Every rumble from on high was a paranoid comment from God, every burst of negative image across the panorama was like a warning from an unknown, mistaken future. The storm screamed at me to go home, to go crawl into a hole and stop pretending I can accomplish anything outside my Habitrail back in Seattle. It's okay to make up fic-tional characters that believe in the portents of the lightning cracks, who hear deities laughing with the bass rumbles of the clouds, but in a personal blog, we are expected to keep things a touch more realistic and rationalized. You're not supposed to advertise your weaknesses and fears to Grandma, and friends you haven't seen in ten years. I guess I don't understand what the audience expects from the format.

She asked me to tell her about my dissertation, so I might as well disgorge it into the webosphere here, where it fits into some conceivable chronology.

I'll explain it sort of like I explained it to Angela.

On August 31, 2005, after finishing summer school at the University of Colorado, I was watching CNN at the student center when they reported on a human stampede event in Baghdad that day.

The war was full-on in Iraq, and over a thousand people were killed during the Shia pilgrimage to the Al-Kadhimiya Mosque when fear of a suicide bomber caused a crowd to try to cross a closed bridge spanning the Tigris River. By all accounts, it ranks as one of the worst crowd crush events in recorded history, although at the time it was barely given a glance by the US news media. There wasn't any footage of the actual crowd event, but what caught my eye that day was the enormous pile of sandals that had been collected into a heap in the aftermath. It was chest-high, and I remember trying to imagine what kind of chaos could have caused that many people to come out of their shoes.

A few years went by and I was back at the school thing, considering dissertation topics for my PhD, when I saw the news about the Love Parade disaster in Duisburg, Germany on July 24, 2010. Twenty-one people died at the music festival when the multitudes of arriving revelers were funneled into a highway underpass tunnel that wasn't big enough for their volume.

Now we're talking about cellphone camera footage of a fatal crowd event as it happened, and the images blew me away. The crowd was mostly stuck, shoulder to shoulder, barely moving, and a few lifeless victims were being passed overhead and lifted out for resuscitation attempts. The scene didn't look like I thought it would. There was no mob rushing in one direction, no bodies being trampled by panicking maniacs. It appeared more or less calm, but people were quietly suffocating at various pressure points because of the slow, forward press and the multiplied hydraulic force of the sea of people around them.

I remember thinking it was amazing, unbelievable, awesomely strange, and horrifying. I was beginning to have problems with agoraphobia, which made the whole thing more disturbing and fascinating, and I considered for the first time looking into the subject as a potential dissertation project. When I saw the footage from Phnom Penh in November, I was convinced that crowd crush was what I wanted to focus my studies on.

At least 347 died when the multitude leaving the Khmer Water Festival got jammed crossing a bridge over the Tonlé Sap River. The madness was caught on multiple video formats, and once again it didn't look like I expected. This time, instead of a calm crowd standing shoulder to shoulder, it was a head-high, tangled pile of slowly struggling and dying Cambodians, and the chaos of rescuers trying to extract bodies—living, dying, and dead—from the enigmatic human knot.

At first I couldn't understand what I was seeing, but horror washed over me when it came into focus. The pile of bodies made no sense and yet it did. Here were echoes of our most gruesome classical representations of Hell. Assorted limbs and torsos and heads, in a hot, writhing, dying heap. Only the ones on top could be removed, and the ones at the bottom were suffocated.

Searching online I found relatively little peer-reviewed work on the science of the stampede phenomenon, and I figured I could come up with a thesis that would combine my background in population statistics with my newfound fascination.

When I read that the pilgrimage to Mecca is the world's number one crowd crush event, I briefly considered researching crowd events that had occurred there at the Jamaraat Bridge, but the travel restrictions against non-Muslims seemed, if not insurmountable, at least prohibitively difficult. Professor Bassoff advised me to expend my dissertation energies wisely and not waste them cutting through Saudi Arabian red tape, so I began looking for locations where I could generate real data. I settled on Duisberg and Jodhpur.

In Germany, I will interview English-speaking survivors of the Love Parade event, make observations of the physical site, and speak with professors Lutz and Boehm from the University of Duisburg-Essen about their data. In India, I will visit the site of the 2008 Chamunda Devi Temple stampede and talk with Professors Reddy and Khanduri from the Indian Institute of Technology. Attempts to locate English-speaking survivors of the Jodhpur event were less successful, but I will still be able to look at the differences between the Eastern and Western methodologies of crowd surge analysis in an attempt to design my Crowd Event Severity and Classification Index.

In order to really crunch some numbers, we need better descriptive tools for the cataloging and analysis of individual incidents, and I'm hoping to come up with a workable methodology. If my model proves useful for research into the prevention of crowd accidents, maybe it will actually assist in saving human lives at some point. The world's population isn't scheduled to peak until around 2050, so it seems pretty good odds that someday, somewhere, my studies will help. It remains to be seen if population increase will bring higher crowd crush incident levels, or if the incident rate will stay the same. In any case, unless the rate drops dramatically—which currently looks unlikely—we can easily imagine many more of these disasters in the future. Thousands of lives might be saved within the next few decades with even a small decrease in fatal stampede events.

As a side project, I'm working on software that will give crowd density estimates using digital photographs and photometrics—another tool that might be used in both research and prevention. I'm imagining a crowd crush warning application for smartphones eventually, including a little warning bell that starts going off at five people per square meter.

Angela listened to me tell her all of this, punctuated poorly by rumbles and flashes above. The wind was warm and made the storm bearable, exotic even after living in the Pacific Northwest for so long, and I wasn't sure if the look on her face was confusion, or fear for my well being, or some mix of the two. I didn't talk about how my growing problems with anxiety disorder made my research laughable, how I wasn't sure I could pull off the next sentence, much less cope with traveling in India, but I think she sensed I was growing uncomfortable and asked about my itinerary.

The energy builds up in the clouds somehow. You can feel it. The sky, the circuits, reach a threshold. This is when the other self shows up with a vajra blast, both in the now and the future, and from somewhere outside myself it all makes sense. Emergence is like the thunder, the lightning. It's everything, but I have to work backward to get there.

My studies keep digging up the emergence concept again and again, no matter what I look into. Every book I pick up lately, every article or paper I read, touches on it somehow, and although it's often disguised by one of its alternate names—the whole that's greater than its parts, synergy, swarm intelligence, flocking, indirect coordination, chaos theory, spontaneous order, self-organizing systems, collective intelligence, paradox, miracle—it's everywhere.

As soon as I looked up "herd behavior," I got into "patterns arising out of the uncoordinated actions of individuals." A twig snaps, or a match lights in the darkness, and an animal reacts with fear, setting off a whole series of events that result in disaster. One after another the cows go over the cliff, victims of what they call an information cascade, everyone making the wrong decision together. I remember at the bottom of that first Wikipedia article, in the See Also section—along with some of the other names for emergence I listed above— anxiety, fear, mass hysteria, and moral panic appeared as links. It was at the bottom of that webpage that I realized my recent social problems and my new interest in crowd crush rubbed up against one another more than a little.

I'm not the first to be mesmerized by a murmuration of starlings, to see in its folding and shape-shifting a shard of the universal, the unknown, the simple adding up to the complex and impossible. The unbearable. Can you separate yourself, your thoughts and actions, from the uncoordinated thoughts and actions of the whole? And if it's not possible to make an individual decision, isn't everything completely out of control, completely fucked? I'm not sure I'm explaining it very well.

Suffice to say, once you start looking in, you discover the other side of serendipity is discordianism, and either everything is significant or nothing is. Not a comfortable place to be.

Talking with another sociology major early last year, she said she didn't understand why I would describe the horror of a human stampede as emergent behavior. She thought the term referred to systems begetting more systems, increasing in complexity, not breaking down. I understood her confusion, or I guess I should say point of view. I wasn't thinking about the people, but the math that described their behavior, and it makes sense to see crowd crush as the opposite of spontaneous order. I told her that just as the butterfly's flutter in one place can eventually cause a storm in another, it usually doesn't. Chaos is not to be confused with randomness. It's everything interconnected playing out in a very specifically fucked way, not unrelated things that happen to have a special moment, and when the whole thing appears to be going backward, there might be a chance to see inside the machinations. I don't think she got it, and sometimes I'm not sure I do.

Everything is emergent from some perspective, and there are no moral phenomena, only interpretations, and truth means little after the stampede. Whether or not there actually is a bomb is irrelevant after the people rush the fence. The injured and dead would still be crushed, no matter the validity of the original declaration about explosives.

Angela said it all sounded so cold and clinical, and asked if I had heard of the local Catalonian tradition of building human towers called *castells*. She said that during certain festivals, groups of castellers have friendly competitions to build the highest human towers, usually crowned by a little boy or girl with a helmet that climbs all the way to the top. She says the crowd pushes in on the men at the base to help them hold back the outward pressure from the human buttresses, and that it makes her think of the opposite of crowd crush, an example of good crowd emergence. We watched a video on her phone, and I was impressed. The same tremendous forces that bust down fences and barricades were being reversed, and were instead supporting a minaret made of men some forty feet tall. She wondered why the running of the bulls in Pamplona seemed comparatively safe next to pilgrimages and entertainment events in other parts of the world. With both bulls and humans stampeding together, the famous San Fermín festival often ends without any serious injuries. What explains the relative safety of the event when it's dangerous by default? She had me there. I'm interested in looking into it more.

We came down from the roof and said our goodbyes in the kitchen, then I walked back through the narrowing streets of the Ciutat Vella to the Gat Chino, where I was relieved to take my sleeping pill. Navigating back on foot through the busy Barcelona night did nothing but wake me up. There's no chance I would have slept without the drug. I watched a few more castelling videos without volume and then I was out, and now—*scroll back down*—the blog emerges while I hide behind this screen in the bustling café. Tiny movements of my fingers become meaning, and reduce potential randomness for a time, while there's an audience—a prospective perspective— until it's forgotten, and the code returns to meaninglessness, entropy.

Brad from Boulder is flying in tomorrow with his fiance and we're taking the train to Montserrat to go rock climbing. My "girlfriend" remains suspiciously unavailable, but again I guess the subject is not travel blog appropriate. I can feel the increased density of everything around me—Europe has more going on per square inch than anywhere I've been lately—and it makes me want more sedatives.

Barcelona's cool, but I'm not feeling especially that way my-self, and I know it will be good to see Brad, and to get up into the mountains. We'll see if there's any Wi-Fi at the campsite, or in the vicinity of the monastery, to type my next update.

Sending.

MONTSERRAT

September 17, 2011

Aeri de Montserrat   bells

Black Virgin   fear of fear

Funicular de Sant Joan   futurephobia

Ignatius of Loyola   Panic and Agoraphobia Scale

Sant Maria de Montserrat Abbey   via dolorosa

The bells are ringing out again from the Abbey of Santa María
de Alaón, and I'm grabbing Wi-Fi at a plastic table outside the
only bar/restaurant on the hill. I guess technically there's the
cafeteria attached to the monastery, but it's for silver-haired
ladies with rosaries, and families with kids. I'm sick of the
sandwiches here, so I might have to join the señoras tomorrow, but they don't have free internet.

On Tuesday, I met up with Brad and Emmy in El Raval, and
they checked into the hostal too, then we had a mellow
evening around the neighborhood. They've both been to
Barcelona before, and Brad said he doesn't give a crap about
the Sagrada Familia, and Gaudí, and Picasso, and panhandlers

dressed up like famous paintings and statues. He wanted rock, and his hands gripped imaginary holds while he talked about it.

We drank Voll-Damms at an outdoor table in Plaça Reial through much of the late afternoon and told stories about undergrad days in Colorado, then we had dinner at a kebab place and did some trip planning. It's good to see Brad again. He's pretty much the funniest guy I know.

Laughter about the old days, the tinkle of carabiners, and the smell of climbing chalk took me back in time, foretelling fun. Brad went on a mission into the darker streets of Chinatown to buy some hash and came back with a chunk in short order. "When in Rome," he said, and rolled up the first of many.

The next morning we took the regional train toward Monistrol from the Plaça d'Espanya station, and only thirty or forty minutes later, we were disembarking at the Monistrol-Aeri station and getting in line for the cable car up to the abbey. I skipped breakfast because I knew we'd be taking the cable car.

After you squeeze into the golden yellow box with twenty other strangers, after the operator slams shut the steel door and locks you all inside with an accented *clunk*, the gondola jumps right into space, right into the clouds, and I ended up enjoying it more than I expected. I imagine everyone but the old man who worked the door felt the same rush as the ground dropped away, everyone's stomach got left behind for a second, and everyone's ears popped within moments. Everyone smiled as we transited out of the mist amid the mountain's magic rock spires, its bands of sheer, serrated cliffs stacked atop each other for miles. I guess it's easier to see discomfort as elation when it's a shared experience.

The cable car takes advantage of some ravines and gullies on Montserrat's flank, flying up about three thousand feet in less than five minutes, to where the Benedictine abbey is tucked away in a small depression beneath the mountain's most impressive rock formations. It is truly a memorable ride. When you get to the top, Santa Maria de Montserrat is surrounded on three sides by magnificent towers of pink-hued, conglomerate stone, while the fourth side of the complex perches on the edge of nothingness with a clear view all the way to Barcelona.

The bells of the chapel were ringing when we exited the cable car, and the effect was impressive. With the huge walls of rock around the bell tower, the tolling rebounded and resonated throughout the maze-work of massive monoliths and hung in the air with rare solidity.

There was camping nearby on one of the paths leading further up the mountain—a well-maintained and traveled *via dolorosa* that winds its way up between crags and along vertiginous drops, with all fourteen stations of the cross, from condemnation to tomb, set at intervals along the way. Most are small relief sculptures set up as shrines in little grottos off the main path, while there are a few that are freestanding or set next to the larger trail.

You check into the camping at the window of a little house perched on the left, and then you're given the keys to a green gate through which you enter the camping area's terraced awesomeness. There isn't a lot of space to work with on the edge of sheer cliffs, so the camp spots consist of a series of ledges connected by steep stairs. An area to play soccer is completely netted over on one end, so the ball doesn't drop two-hundred feet straight down, and even the short walk to the bathrooms includes a vertiginous vista. The bells were already ringing again as we picked out some spots for our tents.

The mellow harmony of the bells marks off every fifteen minutes on most days, with longer soundings on the hour, and on Sundays and special occasions they'll ring them for what seems like forever, a very effective mechanism for making you think about your eternity.

We decided to save the sightseeing for later, and had our hands on the rock before noon. Up close it's a crazy, cobblestoned aggregate with very few cracks, so the game is about holding onto little pebbles that are cemented into the sedimentary substrate.

I can't say it was easy for me, but we ticked off a couple of simple little routes at a crag just a few minutes from the camping area. It had been years since I'd done any climbing, and it was a bit more difficult than I expected.

Brad didn't understand. He said, "Dude, *you* taught *me* how to do this."

My difficulties reminded me of something I read about my agoraphobia, about how the disorder often involves a disruption in the vestibular system, which regulates your balance. I kept silent about it though.

I'm sure it's an experience shared by many visitors, but that first day we laughed every time the bells started up again, which meant we laughed constantly. Brad talked me into smoking some with him on the tip top of a precarious, gold-red needle of stone. We soaked in the sun, and the Catalonian views.

On the top we met some French Canadians and some locals, and the Canadians said that the multi-peaked Montserrat is like Spain's Area 51, a UFO hotspot on the world's ET map. The locals said there is a legend that the one and only Holy Grail is hidden here somewhere too.

I hadn't smoked in some time, and the effects were power-ful but tolerable. While the rest talked about spaceships and extraterrestrial hermits, I kind of blanked out for a while, and saw all kinds of trippy things in the clouds.

On day two, we checked out the abbey and the sanctu-ary, and we got in line to see the famous Black Virgin of Montserrat. Up some stairs in the back of the chapel, inside a glass protective case, on a gilded altar, a Moorish mother of Christ holds an enigmatic, golden orb in her right hand. The sphere sticks out of the case and you're allowed to touch it.

A wooden, Romanesque sculpture from the twelfth century, she is purported to have miraculous powers and goes by var-ious beloved monikers like La Moreneta, Morena de la Serra, and Rosa d'Abril. We were hardly given the opportunity for a spiritual experience with her though because the line had to keep moving. There was a crowd of old ladies with rosaries waiting fervently behind us.

We enjoyed several more days of balmy climbing around Los Gorros, and L'Elefant, and Panxa del Bisbe—always within earshot of the sounding bells—and on the third morning Brad and Emmy headed down to the little town of Monistrol to get groceries while I headed off by myself to the top of the peak called Sant Jeroni.

The Funicular de Sant Joan is an inclined railway that takes people from the abbey level to the top of Sant Jeroni. I shared the little green car with some dreadlocked rock rats and middle-aged German tourists. I started to get uncomfortable with myself during the ratcheted ride—maybe it was the way the interior of the train-car itself was built sloped at forty degrees to accommodate the extreme incline. Entering it is like going into one of those crooked houses they have at amusement parks, where perspective and angles are tweaked so everything seems impossible, where water poured from a jug goes off to the side instead of streaming straight down.

I failed to recognize the premonitory sensory phenomena again. Many afflicted with agoraphobia learn to recognize the approach of an attack. Some describe it as an urge, which they say is semi-voluntary, whatever that means. No two sufferers experience it the same way, but most receive subtle clues preceding an episode.

When I got to the top, I should have paid attention to how I was feeling on the funicular. If I had paid attention, I probably wouldn't have gone and found a private spot to smoke some hash. As it happens, I ignored the signals, and when the bells started up again things went critical—I fucking lost it.

Tucked into a little nook in the labyrinth of stone, I thought I had escaped the bells and was alone, but other voices channeled through the complex landscape, and I couldn't help feeling like someone was with me, or watching me. What followed could be lifted right off the Wikipedia page for agoraphobia: pounding heart, sweating, shaking, problems breathing, nausea, dizziness, feeling of losing control/going crazy.

From my almost-cave, I could see one chunk of sky, and the clouds inside it spiraling out into a thing like a serpent with dark areas resembling eyes, but then it turned into a piece of flowing fabric, like a scarf, and I saw writing on it that I couldn't make out.

I heard the bells again, but the sound changed. They weren't glorious anymore but turbulent and clamorous. They screamed at me about my own stupidity, my worthlessness. Marking off my madness every quarter hour, they mocked me, singing, "The clock keeps ticking and nothing has changed. The clock keeps ticking and nothing has changed."

I'm an ulcer. I'm the piece of shit at the center of the universe. I'm the Travelocity gnome's boring owner. We've all seen that cute movie in which he eventually leaves home, but we know it doesn't happen like that in real life. He never went anywhere because if he did *this* would happen. He would freak out and hide himself in a fucking hole.

The fabric in the sky wrapped itself into something like a hive. It was like imaginary hands grabbed my throat from behind and I couldn't shrug them off. The bells stopped their frantic chiming but the beehive in the sky continued to bombinate, a throbbing that I heard but was sure did not exist.

My therapist told me not to "outsource control to the environment," and I kept thinking about trying to keep my shit together while walking back to the main path. I wanted Maxwell Smart's Cone of Silence, so I could be in my own little world while in public, but that doesn't exist yet. I wished for my phone, even though it doesn't work here, so I could act like I was texting.

When I made it to the place where Jesus drops his cross for the second time, I lost it for the second time too. There was a small group of tourists looking at the carving, one of them asked me something I didn't understand, I turned away embarrassed and confused, and the whole thing started over again: the symptoms, the bells, and me finding a hole to hide in. This time it was accompanied by more religious iconography. All the Jesuses.

Calling someone the son of God used to mean they had no proper father. Jesus was a bastard just like most of the rest of us, and he went on to kill himself by letting himself be killed anyway, at least until he was resurrected. What are we supposed to make of it? And it's always Our Lady of the Blessed This or That, and never Our Lady of the Compromised Position, or Our Lady of the Malignant Growth, or Saint Verde, patron saint of jealousy.

I returned to more or less normal before I noticed a guy sitting on a rock nearby. He startled me. I didn't know how long he had been there but he looked like just another young climber dude. He waved politely, and then he said, "*Eres uno de nosotros.*"

I understood his Spanish—you're one of us—but not what he meant. He said people come here to hide, that it's the history of this place.

It was to be my first real conversation in Spanish on this trip. The truth is, I've made many visits to Spain because of my father, but I've never made easy connections with Spaniards. It's like I feel extra introverted in a culture of extroverts, and I can't really roll my r's, or conjugate my verbs very well, although my mild lisp works okay here. I can't even say my own name like they say it here.

In any case, Sancho introduced himself, and seemed to understand that I was having a bad time. He said this place is all about people seeking refuge from the bigger world, that the mountaintop is covered with the abandoned hovels of reclusive monks. He said I must know of Loyola, but wasn't surprised when I said I didn't.

He was right though, I *had* heard of the Jesuits, and he explained to me that it was here that the founder of that religious order had his first spiritual visions, after which he laid down—or maybe it was hung up—his weapons and retreated to a cave nearby in Manresa.

In English, he's best known as Ignatius of Loyola, but you can call him Ignacio as well, or because he was a Basque, you might as well call him by his name in Euskara, Iñigo Loiolakoa, but Sancho preferred to call him Iggy for my sake.

The big deal about Iggy was that he came up with a series of spiritual exercises through which the pupil works to improve their relationship with God. Sancho said that to a modern non-Christian much of it wasn't very interesting, but what *was* cool was that Iggy was actually teaching people to meditate.

Iggy got hit by a cannonball in the battle for Pamplona in 1521, and while he was recovering, he read this book called *De Vita Christi* which taught him about methods of "simple contemplation." Essentially, by envisioning yourself somewhere else, and by trying to take in imaginary details of that place through all five senses, you can reach a place of spiritual calm or advancement. These days, we all know this kind of thing from elementary school, when the teacher makes everyone close their eyes and visualize something, but in the 1520's, this was some radical, borderline heretical stuff.

Of course most of Iggy's visualization exercises involve contemplating various important scenes from the life of Jesus, but some of them get pretty wacky. Sancho said exercise number five is a meditation on Hell, and that there's one in the appendix that contains *reglas para el discernimiento de los espíritus*—rules for the discernment of spirits.

He said that beyond spirits, the discernment thing was interesting in and of itself. Apparently Iggy truly believed in angels and demons, that they're always all around us, trying to guide us or trick us, that God and the Devil are active players, and the key to making proper decisions in this haunted reality involves the semi-mystic process of "discernment."

Essentially anytime you make a choice in the world, you are either cooperating with God or you aren't, and if you've been meditating and paying attention to the life of Jesus, you will be better equipped to make the decision in line with God's grace, in which case you share in that grace a tiny bit, making every one of life's decisions a potentially mystic process at the same time that it is a real and normal decision.

Sancho laughed and said no wonder Iggy stayed in a cave seven hours a day, he was too caught up in the whole free will conundrum to make a decision about anything. Luckily, he said, Gödel has proved more recently that there are explanatory feedback loops in all systems, and most of us don't worry about the existence of choice anymore.

Nevertheless, he said, it is puzzling to consider the nature of choice, how every one of us is Maxwell's demon heating up God-only-knows what, and from there it was tortoises all the way down, *et sic in infinitum*. I said I didn't understand about the turtles, and he said it wasn't important, that philosophy is just a way to organize your monsters, and you can vectorize the analogy—make it infinitely expandable or reducible.

Moving on, he said that on a larger scale what was really happening back then was that people were attacking old concepts with this recently resurrected stuff called logic, and the

Church had to come up with logical ways to bring people back in. Meditating worked for many adherents, so the methods were accepted, even though they smacked of inappropriate, Eastern mysticism.

He said Abrahamic religions have no way to deal with the fact that inside what we believe there exists the opposite of what we believe. He said you could also look at it along the lines of noise versus signal, but then he said the whole thing is being held together by illusions anyway, and that it was better not to think about it.

He said Iggy had it right in some ways though—just go be by yourself for a while and think about something else.

All of this made me feel better and worse. I walked back down the mountain thinking about some of the things I would have said to Sancho if I had spoken stronger Spanish.

For one thing, Loyola's spiritual exercises reminded me of the Panic and Agoraphobia Scale, or PAS, a self-administered, online examination that my therapist has me take once a week so we can monitor my situation. Apparently the test itself can have therapeutic effects, especially when you're doing better than you thought you were. Being forced to look back at the week and add it all up is a form of meditative visualization, even if I'm not imagining I'm Christ.

The test starts off simple enough. *How frequent and severe were your attacks?* Then it gets into counting how many things you've avoided during the week because of your fear of an attack. And

then it gets more difficult by asking you to rate the importance
of the events you have avoided. Maybe it's just me, but the
importance of one thing over another seems to dissipate under
any sort of honest scrutiny. After that the test gets rather enigmatic by asking if you've experienced the "fear of fear," and by
having you rate your fear of fear. The last question on the test—
technically it's two questions—is a doozy, and worth quoting in
full: "Did you sometimes believe that your doctor was wrong
when he told you your symptoms have a psychological cause?
Do you believe that in reality a somatic cause lies behind these
symptoms that hasn't yet been found?"

Beyond the obvious problems separating body from mind
and vice versa, this type of loaded interrogative sounds like
the doctor slipping in an advertisement for himself at the end
of the session, like the message is that you really are crazy
for feeling the way you do, and you better keep seeing your
doctor. God help you if you believe angels and demons are
interfering in your personal life. There's no box to check if you
believe your symptoms have a divine or diabolical cause.

I'll bet old Iggy would have failed the PAS test miserably. He
hid out in a cave all the time, and would definitely be advised
to seek therapy and be put on medications these days. There's
got to be quite a bit in common between mental patients and
mystics.

It's hard to be certain how they would diagnose him, or anyone on the continuum from shut-in to shy. The fuzzy, overlapping definitions and categorizations tend to confuse rather
than clarify.

Agoraphobia is classified by the *Diagnostic and Statistical Manual of Mental Disorders* as a subset of anxiety disorder, but once you start reading about anxiety, it is differentiated from panic, and while anxiety might lead to panic, there are a good percentage of panic attacks not preceded by anxiety. Pinning the definition down seems difficult from the start.

According to the DSM, panic disorder comes with or without its sidekick agoraphobia, and you either have panic attacks when you go certain places, or you have them for other reasons. If you start avoiding events or places because you're scared you'll have a panic attack, then you're an agoraphobe.

Because the word is ostensibly Greek, it's easy to imagine ancient philosophers struggling to classify the disease like we do today, but the word *agoraphobia* was made up for the syndrome in 1871 by an Austrian psychiatrist named Carl Otto Westphal, and as far as we know, Plato and Socrates never placed the Greek word for "marketplace" in front of the suffix for "fear" during their dialogues.

To Westphal, the concept was intimately connected to space because it was the fear of places that he observed in his patients. But most modern therapists approach it differently because it's not so much the place that is feared as it is what might happen there—the increased embarrassment and terror of a panic attack outside one's "safety zone."

That said, there are many agoraphobes whose fear of places or spaces is not connected to the fear of fear feedback loop, and still many more whose avoidances are caused by social instead of spatial phobias. There are some, the enochlophobes, who are specifically scared of crowds, not places, and the exceptions and singularities go on and on. In the end, each agoraphobe has his own individual head game that resists easy identification. We'll never know for sure what was going on with Iggy, whether his fears were of this kind or of another.

Many therapists want to link agoraphobia to a thought process that they think they can adjust, whereas to the sufferer the syndrome is a physical thing. Anyone familiar with the habits of our primitive cousins, the rodents, knows they prefer not to cross wide, open spaces. This is a programmed evolution-ary advantage against predation. I believe that with humans, agoraphobic reactions are the electrochemical surfacing of forgotten instincts. The thought process, like so often in life, is just ornamentation. I don't deny that reverse engineering can work—tinkering with the thought to remove the symp-toms—but it reminds me of that old line about moving the hands on the clock to try and fix the gears inside.

And right on time the bells again. They sound solemn now. Not mad, but melancholy, monotone.

I looked for Brad and Emmy at the campground, but they weren't around, and I can't say I really wanted to get right to explaining my freak out to them anyway, so I went to the bar with my laptop instead of waiting at the tents. Add another avoidance to the week's tally.

Because I've never talked to them about it, they're going to want to know my symptoms, my history, my meds, and I could go through the humiliation of explaining it to them face to face, or I guess I could just politely tell them to read this blogpost instead.

As far as the meds go, you've got your SSRIs, your MAO inhibitors, your tricyclic antidepressants. You can take Sertraline, Paroxetine, Fluoxetine, benzodiazepine, and the list goes on. I've settled on a careful combination of Paxil and Xanax, mostly.

For therapies, there's systematic desensitization or in vivo exposure, and there's cognitive restructuring, and relaxation techniques. My counselor doesn't do anything out of the ordinary—he hasn't gone with me to crowded places and coached me through it or anything—we just talk about it mostly. He tries to steer me away from my more philosophical wanderings on the subject, but we occasionally make forays into agoraphobia's enigmas.

I soon got over the circular nature of the "panic attacks are caused by panic attacks" argument, but it was strange when I realized it wasn't the places that I feared but what might happen there. Eventually, I found it to be in line with my thoughts on our rodent nature, because what the rat really abhors is the hawk and the owl, not the open field.

Still stranger was wrestling with where concepts of the "self" overlap, conflict, and interact with the disease. Think Eastern religious ideas of "oneness," or consider Derrida saying that the determination of the self "as one" is violence. The split between the thing and everything else, the lonely god creating something to accompany him, the division between the

person and the pack—what is alone is what is alone, and anyone with agoraphobia knows that whether you fear the crowd
or not, the panic attack singles you out among the masses.

And, no surprise, along the topic of alone, Lydia hasn't an-
swered any of my attempts to call or Skype her in a week—silence—and I'm pretty sure I don't have a girlfriend anymore.
I'm trying to avoid the subject in the blog, but what the fuck?

The bells again.

I upped my dosage with the last beer and they sound old and
rusty now, almost muffled. God screams and does mad pirou-
ettes while they groan for all our eventual deaths.

My therapist says that, really, what agoraphobes are scared
of is death, that we all suffer necrophobia, death being the
"ultimate separation from the safety zone," but I wonder if we
reach deeper down, past death, to causation itself and the sequential nature of reality—the things that death is made of—I
wonder if actually it's the future that we fear, because nothing
can ever be unstirred again. Working backward is impossible.

Oddly enough, there's no Greek compound for fear of the
future, no futurephobia, even though What Is To Come by
definition includes all the horror and terror of all the other
phobias combined.

Sending.

ARENAS DE CABRALES

September 21, 2011

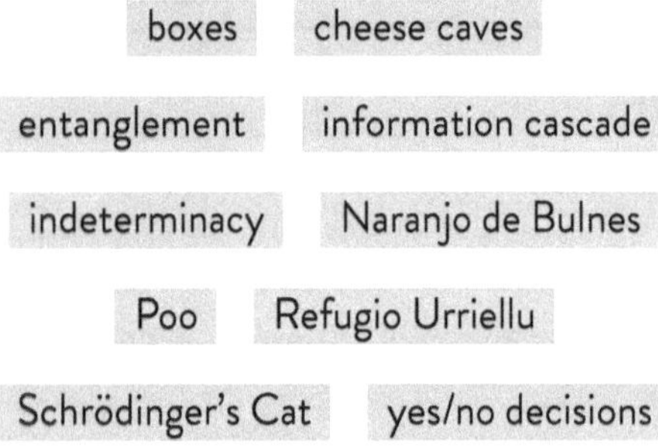

First, you open a new window to place the narrative some-where. Let's call it a box instead, because windows are not generally used to contain things. Whether we're creating a file, or deciding on a new blog template, we're taking out a box for whatever it is, and determining what should be put in it.

In this box, I'm in the restaurant/bar at the campground just outside the town of Arenas de Cabrales. I'm sitting at a table with my laptop and a bottle of the house red—cheaper than bottled water here. Depending on the size you make the box, and the resolution of your monitor, you might be able to see how much wine remains in the bottle.

But you don't know how I got here in this little box, so let's open another box to share the screen with the first one.

In the second one, we see me and Brad and Emmy leaving Barcelona on an overnight train bound for Oviedo after a week of rock climbing at Montserrat. We are transiting autonomous communities from Catalonia to Asturias, on the way to what's kind of like Spain's Yosemite, Los Picos de Europa, and our ultimate goal, Naranjo de Bulnes, one of Iberia's most famous summits, known to the locals as Picu Urriellu.

Before continuing, we should be able to go ahead and open a third box here.

In this rectangle, we see the payphone near the laundry machines at the campgrounds, and me standing there dialing numbers off a prepaid phone card.

We could add more, but three seems manageable for now. Of course I have no control over what windows or boxes you already have open on your monitor, sharing space with mine. It could be a search engine, or a spreadsheet. A Progressive ad or a porn site. The possibilities approach infinity.

I have no idea ahead of time what the promotions or commercials in the margins of my blog post will say, and whether or not they will be congruent with my commentary. Maybe they will complement it, or perhaps they will seem in poor taste. Either way, I ask you, the reader, to look now and see what's next to this, what's behind it, interrupting or overlapping it. Take a screenshot here. Take a souvenir.

It's tempting to open a fourth box that demonstrates the narrative as I would have liked it to happen, but I've decided to stick with reality. If necessary, I can call it the *theoretical* fourth box. We'll be coming back to theoretical boxes.

Whether it's colored dots of red, yellow, and green, or a minus sign, a square inside a square, and an X, pick the appropriate key, click, or gesture to return to the second frame.

We got tickets for the sleeper car thinking it would be fun to snooze on the train, but the top bunks where Brad and Emmy were assigned had zero ventilation, and the air inside our rolling metal chamber had to be well over a hundred degrees. We retreated to the bar car and drank cans of Estrella beer until they closed it down past midnight, then we spent most of the wee hours hanging out next to the open windows in the passageway, sneaking the occasional hash cigarette.

Arriving in Oviedo mid morning, we had bocadillos de jamon at your typical, old school, Spanish hole-in-the-wall, bought some provisions at a *supermercado*, and made our way to the bus terminal downtown, where we got on a regional bus bound for Cabrales.

Brad thought it might help me relax if we got tanked on cheap wine during the bus ride, but we failed to appreciate the length of the slow, winding highway, and the bathroom's "*Fuera de Servicio*" signage. Before we reached Cangas de Onís, Brad cut open the top of the empty wine carton and filled it to the very rim again with urine. We were at the back so nobody saw.

I had to piss so bad it hurt to laugh, and when we finally got off
the bus in Arenas it was hard to walk. Emmy was completely
embarrassed, and told us she liked our college camaraderie,
but that we weren't in college anymore.

The town might be described as nondescript by Asturian stan-
dards, but as it sits along several meanders of the Rio Cares,
nestled between the emerald foothills and the first rocky
flanks of the Picos, the view is impressive once you've drained
your bladder.

The region is famous for its cheese, which is often cured in
caves. The caves are numerous here because the massifs are
mostly limestone, and there's even a cheese cave tour at the
edge of town. After centuries of occupation and production,
the caves have been outfitted with doors and windows and
floors, and all the other etcetera of modernity, so that while
the walls are still rock, the spaces within look more like base-
ments than caverns.

When we walked past the tour signs, I was reminded of my
freak-outs in Montserrat the week before, when my panic
attacks made me hide in the rocks. I realized that now that we
were in Asturias, where everything is green and moist, like back
in northwest Washington, I almost felt comfortable in my skin.

As we walked the road along the river toward the campground, I wondered if the cheeses in the caves were the
chickens or the eggs. Considering my recent struggles with
agoraphobia, it didn't seem far-fetched to propose that the
proto-Asturianos were already hiding in the caves when they

developed the cheese, and not the other way around. I doubt they sought out the caves to make cheese.

We picked the camping area outside Arenas because of its proximity to the peak we were after, and it shares the mountain's moniker in a matter-of-fact manner: Camping Naranjo de Bulnes. The tent sites are along the river, a little path goes past cherry trees down to its edge, and upon our first exploration of it, I found nothing incongruous with the small rivers of the Puget Sound region, except for an eel hovering in the shadow of a rock. I had never seen an eel in the wild before.

There are bathrooms and shower buildings on both sides of the road, and the one on the Bulnes side has a laundry area and a row of increasingly endangered payphones. These phones provide some degree of privacy away from the bar and other campers, and it is these I planned to use to call my so-called girlfriend again—from which I will eventually try to open the metaphorical, theoretical box.

Minimize this one, maximize that one.

We planned to overnight at the refuge near the base of the climb, and we learned of bunks and food available there, so we were able to lighten our loads by leaving one of our tents set up at the campground with all of our extraneous gear in it.

The weather was questionable when we set out for a steep day hike to the peak, and by the time we got through the irregularly cobblestoned section of trail beyond the tiny town of Bulnes, and up into the high, grassy hills, the famous Asturian clouds had made up their barometric decision and released their rain on our vicinity. We knew we had a place to dry out for the night, so we soldiered onwards soaked, past various types of Spanish sheep, and the slopes they'd been summering on for centuries. We passed tiny, stone cottages still occupied by shepherds during the nice months, one of which advertised in a hand-scrawled sign on cardboard, "*Se Vende Queso.*"

Brad asked me at some point about my last attempt to phone "Whatshername," and when I told him the call went to voicemail again he said he suspected that the cat was dead. Emmy snorted a little, then hit Brad in a way that meant he should be more sensitive.

When I asked what he meant, he said that the inquiry into the situation affects the situation, like the famous thought experiment with the cat in the box. Whether or not I still have a girlfriend represents the indeterminacy, only discoverable by looking inside the container, and the process of looking in forces it to be alive or dead.

When I said I had never really gotten the Schrödinger's cat thing, Emmy said, "Brad has tried to explain it to me a thousand times and I still don't understand." Then she said, "Change that to still don't *care.*"

I asked Brad for a refresher.

"It all started when Young destroyed the corpuscular theory of light with his two-slits experiment," he said. "These guys studying tiny particles started getting into whether or not their observations were changing the results."

Emmy chimed in, "Like, how can you see if the refrigerator light is on when the door's closed?"

Brad said not quite, and Emmy retorted that he himself had used the fridge example in the past. He was forced to explain that Schrödinger's cat was a thought experiment *like* the fridge thing, but was not analogous. Then he continued.

"The results these guys were getting were demonstrating what was eventually referred to as *verschränkung*, or entanglement. Einstein called it *spukhafte Fernwirkung*, or spooky action at a distance.

"Particles separated by space still affected each other although no connection could be proven between them. The numbers demonstrated it, but the fact was difficult to swallow, and Schrödinger came up with a thought experiment to describe what he saw as a contradiction in quantum theory as it was emerging.

"He and Einstein had an ongoing dialogue about it. Essentially you've got something random like a roll of the dice determining whether or not the mechanism kills the cat, and from outside the closed container you can quantify the situation by saying the cat is some percentage value of alive or dead. So accepting the new quantum equations was like saying the cat can be alive *and* dead simultaneously, which we know isn't how things really work, except that *is* how things really work on the subatomic level—at least when you're trying to explain it."

Then he said that *my* cat's probably just plain dead though.

After a few moments of the three of us hiking in the heavy rain without saying anything, he added that Einstein preferred using a keg of black-powder to blow up the theoretical cat, while Schrödinger preferred to poison it with cyanide gas.

Emmy said it reminded her of the passage in the book *The Little Prince* where the narrator is asked to draw a sheep, but he has difficulty sketching it correctly, so he draws a box instead and says the sheep is inside the box.

Brad said he sort of saw what she meant, and that for sure it all boils down to perspective.

"What they were talking about was whether or not to accept a blurred model of reality, because that was all they were being given. Schrödinger compared it to the difference between an out-of-focus picture that looked like fog or clouds, and an actual photograph of fog or clouds. Only one of them is the real deal."

I wondered exactly *what* was being compared to the difference between the two photos, but I didn't go there. Instead I suggested we take a picture of the clouds that we were walking through.

Brad kept going, and said Einstein said that reality is

something independent of what is experimentally established. I remember sort of fading out while he spieled on about wave functions, and superposition, and eigenstates, but finally he brought it back around and said it often breaks down to what's up between Alice and Bob, a pair of metasyntactic variables living in the mythical realm of Ruritania. My relationship, or lack of relationship, with Whatshername might be expressed as an equation.

While Brad's brain loved this stuff, it had never been easy for me, and I wondered if it made any sense to wonder if there was a quantum relationship between being wanted and being had.

After some more quiet hiking in the rain, Emmy said she thought it was important to visualize the cat as alive.

"Besides," she said, "it's kind of like Pascal's wager or whatever, because there's nothing to lose, right?"

She tended toward hope, while my mind was wont to turn any discussion about physics into thoughts about bodies in crowds. I couldn't help but liken entanglement to emergence. Although a flock of birds is composed of individuals making independent decisions, the group seems to move as one—sort of like the particles that once interacted, got separated, and then continued to influence each other across seemingly empty space.

I know I'm not the only one thinking about this stuff. They did a story on NPR a few months ago about some young particle physicists who love metal music and mosh pits, and who see parallels between the rules of movement in oscillating atomic elements, and the ways people are shoved around at rowdy concerts. A person in a crowd is simultaneously an individual and part of a crowd. This brings with it all the usual philosophical breakdowns.

Brad said Schrödinger's whole thing was a *reductio ad absurdum* argument anyway, reckoning that the conclusion is false because it's absurd.

"Not tight logic," he said. "New research suggests that human consciousness evolved out of the quantum interactions going on in our brain, so there's little luck it's something we'll ever be able to explain." What's really cool, he said, is that they're describing subatomic particles more and more like packets of information. Minute yes-or-no decisions that the entire universe is constructed of.

I watched the raindrops exploding on the rocks—each one a tiny verdict, a minuscule judgment.

The frame of reference might suddenly come into question and dissolve, dropping you back into a different place. Like software crashing, one box disappears and reveals the one beneath it. We're at the table in the restaurant again with the bottle of wine and an error message.

Just like these guys come up with math models to explain things otherwise unexplainable, I'll write about it like I understand what's going on so my theoretical reader can think they get it too. And this abstract audience is the same as the observer in the laboratory, fucking with my experiment, making a joke out of the results. Nobody can explain anything, and that's exactly the point.

We start as children trying to fathom language and the world, and from early on we learn to pretend to understand, wanting to be like the grownups. But the thing is, our parents don't really get it either, they just have an adult version of not understanding. That's what the cat thing comes down to. More mature stratagems for expressing utter ignorance.

I'm pretty sure the girl that works behind the bar thinks I'm an idiot too. There are little gnome-like figurines peculiar to Asturias standing around the cash register, and when I asked what they're called in Spanish she looked annoyed. She said, "*Enanitos*," then walked away while checking her phone. She looks about nineteen, and she probably feels trapped working at her family's restaurant in this comparative Nowheresville. Perhaps she'll realize this is paradise years from now.

Anyway, restore the collapsed narrative.

We remained within the clouds and rain, the terrain got steeper, and we were channeled into stone gullies that wound up past pillars, cliffs, and talus fields, until we arrived at Refugio de Urriellu in the late afternoon. We were beyond soaked. Only once did the sky slide open for a few seconds to reveal what was to be our white whale, the trapezoidal monolith suddenly towering in blue above us, like God opening the box that we're in for a moment. Like we were glancing up at the laboratory lights and the scientist's shadow, and then the box was closed again.

First we came across some campsites among large boulders—tents set up throughout a small basin, like satellites of the refuge—then the building itself emerged from the fog, perched directly below what would be the impressive, west side of the 550 meter wall, if the clouds didn't exist.

The refuge is a large, two-level stone structure assembled of rocks collected from the close vicinity, and the face of the much older, smaller shelter was preserved when the building was expanded, leaving in place the hand-hewn arches above the front entry so that one can see the evidence of its metamorphosis.

Because it had been raining all day, the place was crowded with climbers, and while I was relieved to get out of my wet things, we went from being alone in the wilderness to inside a congested trans-European hangout by simply ducking underneath its low front door. After checking in, I was overwhelmed and wanted to go back outside, but all my gear was already hanging up to dry, so I retreated as soon as possible to the bunkroom upstairs, got inside my bag, and swallowed a sleeping pill. The grumble of assorted dialects slowly transmogrified into unremembered dreams.

The next day we waited in the clouds wearing damp clothes, and we agreed that if the weather was still poor on the second morning we would head back to Arenas instead of holding out another day. We took little smoking excursions through

the mists in the shallow valley—at least it wasn't raining—and
chatted with other climbers on the front patio, and at the
booths in the dining hall. At some point, Emmy asked me how
I was doing, and she sort of got into the whole I'm-worried-
about-you thing. She was especially concerned about how I
was going to deal with India later in the trip. I said I doubted
that her bringing it up could make it easier in any way, and
she apologized, then I apologized. She wondered if there was
a connection between my early interests in climbing, and the
onset of agoraphobia later in my life, then she said she meant
more of a progression than a connection, or that people who
tend toward escapism early on in life might be more prone
to social disorders later on. I had never looked at it like that
before, and I thought some more about it while wandering
around in the fog, which I found comforting once I got out of
the vicinity of the refuge. Perhaps it was like feedback from
my meds, a fog on fog resonance. Harmonic tranquilization.

On the second morning in the refuge, the clouds persisted,
and one of the staff said the forecast was more rain, so for
the first half of the return trip, we hiked in the same massive
blanket of water vapor that we had been snuggled beneath for
days. Then blue and green came back to us around the midway
point and laughed at our retreat. While we could no longer see
the central massif from our vantage, we saw bright skies above
it, and that's just the way it goes. The rain probably cleared up
because we were watching it.

The way back was mostly downhill, and we returned to the
campground early in the afternoon with relatively high spirits
despite Urriellu's rejection of us. After a hot shower, I tried

calling Lydia again, which slides us back into box number three, the view of the payphones next to the laundry area.

I finally got the thing open to discover the cat had been dead for quite some time.

Does the observation still affect the event when the thing went down weeks ago, and the corpse has been rotting inside the contraption ever since?

At least I released some flies from captivity.

She's been fucking somebody else the whole time I've been gone. How's that for an appropriate blog topic?

The particle decayed, the gas was released, or the barrel of gunpowder exploded. The cat was stiff as a board, maggot-infested, or blown to bits. It's been chopped into little pieces by a mad scientist, or a redneck threw it out on the side of the road and popped the clutch on it. It's been eviscerated, decapitated, turned inside out, and crucified. Burned at the stake, tortured, and shat on. An imbecile jerked off all over it after strangling it. It was so fucking dead that it never even fucking existed.

What do they do in their thought experiment with the inevitable corpse?

I tried to hurt the phone when I hung up, then I just started walking.

From the campground on Highway 114, it's about a kilometer to Arenas proper, and I entered and exited the town without realizing what I was doing. My feet moved unwittingly and the landscape moved past me. The river, the rapids, and the cliffs meant nothing to me. The speed limit increased, and the cars ripped by at a good clip an arm's length away.

No other pedestrians stomped this section of road, and that was just fine by me. I considered how easy it would be to step out into the path of a truck.

The information cascade hit my brain like the proverbial tsunami, like the footage of the Tōhoku event this March in Japan, a wall of water sweeping across all the Xs and Ys and Zs and obliterating the lot, pushing an enormous, churning bulk-head of debris, presided over by the Angel of History. All of my hope, optimism, faith, trust, and confidence smashed and drowned forward and backwards through time. What I had was garbage, what I have is wreckage, what I will have is ruins.

Clarity and my ability to recall came intermittently, with huge holes in the visual field. Like the Streetview feature of Google's mapping, you can't see from every angle or position, the vantage is only capable of leapfrogging between particu-lar coordinates, and from there it can only spin in horizontal circles, not down to the ground or up to the sky.

After several kilometers of despair, I appreciated the road sign that heralded the next little hamlet down the highway. On a white field with a red border, it said the one simple word, "Poo," and while I'm sure it's pronounced differently

in Spanish, it sure looked like shit to me. At that moment
the name seemed more than appropriate, and I kept walking
through Poo as assorted wreckage continued to surface in the
froth atop the data deluge, before getting sucked under again.

Let's go *Full Screen* on the things that float to the top.

A late-night conversation with her in my kitchen when we
first met. She said she likes to fix broken things, and I wondered if what's implied is that she breaks them.

On the radio, they talked about a rare disease called Williams
syndrome. Because of a genetic mutation, its sufferers love
and trust other people without discrimination. Morning light
came through the window, and she was still asleep on the bed
next to me. I wondered if she had the disease.

At a burrito place in the University District, we skirted around
the monogamy topic, and she said something about the slippery slope to nowhere, then she giggled and winked and said
hope is at its best when things are at their worst.

The light from her phone lit the way for us as we trespassed
afterhours in the Washington Park Arboretum, and I remembered the blue-white light on her face. After living for a few
years in the cell-service backwater of the San Juan Islands,
she was my first cellphone girlfriend, and I marveled at the
unexpected illumination from her gadget.

With her in the window seat fuming at me, and the city going
by behind her outside the bus, I considered the differences

between problems caused by things you've done, and problems caused by things you haven't, and I observed that it was
difficult enough being happy without her.

In the early days of our relationship, someone told me that to
ensure happiness with her, I had to reduce expectations and
approach the thing sideways, and in the wee electric glow of
my increasingly anachronistic alarm clock, with her deepen-
ing breath demonstrating her progress towards dreamworld,
I wondered just how one went about approaching goals
latitudinally.

Box number four—full of things that could have been—comes
to the surface for a second before getting submerged again.

The wreckage continued to get pushed further ashore.
Tumbled, churned, and dumped in my memory, destroying
pretty things from the past by heaping them together with
the shitstorm, the sewage, the sludge. The turds put in the
Cuisinart with the fruit. Since everything supposedly boils
down to perspective, I could choose to look at the tidal wave
as a liberator, a beautiful awakening, a revelation, but I know
myself, and it's probably personally impossible.

Exit Full Screen.

What's left will inevitably spill over into text. There will be
angry emails with supplemental accusations, extraneous
justifications, and the advertisements in the margins of the
pages will infuriate me. Now if you write about relationships
or breakups, the most intimate details of your precious love

and its pathetic dissolution get run through the algorithm like
everything else you type, and the promotions that paral-
lel your correspondence will peddle self-help books for the
brokenhearted, ringtones for the forlorn, love potions for the
forsaken. The nouns from all your problems get run through
the equation like everything else, so they can sell you exactly
what you need. So far I've never seen any real solution offered
up in the sidebar.

What does it do to the "appropriate audience" concept when
the majority of your "readers" might be programs designed to
market things to you? Isn't it strange to be concerned about
who's perusing your blog, and what details from your private
life might be too personal for the internet, when the lot of
it has already been absorbed and dissected by commercial
robots?

I don't really want to share with my grandmother or my uncle
about my girlfriend fucking someone else, but it seems silly to
worry about it when Big Brother 2.0 already knows, and even
offers assistance, albeit in the form of products I will never
purchase, aligned on the perimeters of the page.

Perhaps the best way to unbox it all without having to exclude
people is to make up another self, another dude and his blog.
If you don't want to tell the whole world about your Dear
John phone call but you still want to let it out, just fashion
an alternate persona, and post it in his travelogue. Details to
embellish the story may be collected from the internet, and
no one needs to know that the author never went anywhere.
In fact, they would probably prefer not to.

A speck of dust on my display occults a screensaver star, and I realize I'm drifting off. The waitress is gone somewhere, the bottle is empty, and it's just me and the enanitos here in the restaurant. I wake up the computer, and consider deleting this whole post, or at least punching *Command+Q*.

Click on the corners and make the other two boxes disappear. You can close them, put them away, but it doesn't stop you from thinking about what's in them. You can file things away all neat and tidy on a computer, but it doesn't work like that in your brain.

Then at some point—no matter how you look at it—you've got to close this box too.

Sending.

GIJÓN

September 27, 2011

Crowds and Power   crusades

Elias Canetti   La Loca

Museo Internacional de La Gaita   paranoiac continuum

Reconquista   Revillagigedo Palace

School of Salamanca   types of crowds

When you begin writing the entry already knowing how it ends, do you start with the best of it? Do you package it for maximum effect, or just get it over with? Do you start with the cleanup from the previous post's tsunami, or get into how the anxieties are making incursions against the drugs?

If I explain that I'm getting worried about how I'm going to manage traveling in India, or I hint at the possibility of another panic attack, does it build suspense, or does it sound too much like exposition? I will repeat that the "cat" from the previous posts is beyond dead, and what's the point of bringing up a rotten cat. She will not be mentioned again soon.

Because of the way a blog stacks up, once you get into it

some distance it starts to go the other way. If the beginning becomes the end and vice versa, then somewhere in the middle is where it reverses direction. Like a slack tide, balanced, anticipating the turn. But whether it's coming in or going out, the water is falling. If water had feelings it would usually feel like it's falling. Right now, from the kitchen window here, I can see outside to the beach, and the waves are making their slow, oscillating advance up the sand.

My father rents a place in Gijón every summer now. He makes sure he's here for most of September, when the weather in Asturias is at its best. This summer's is a typical Spanish apartment, with low ceilings and small furniture, and plenty of knickknacks to remind you that nautical kitsch isn't strictly an American phenomenon.

Dad still has friends and family in Gijón—a couple of childhood buddies, and a few cousins—and his activities here consist mostly of journeys to the beach when the sun is out, and walks along the promenade, El Muro, which continues next to the water from Parque del Cerro to Parque de El Rinconín. For the most part that's what my activities with Dad will consist of, walks along the arch of the bay, participating in the town parade that never seems to end during the nice months. My father links his fingers behind his back while he walks, and fits in more here than anywhere else in the world. The other old men sound and stroll just like him.

I can't say I feel as confident in my strides, or that I feel like I fit in. Since I arrived here a few days ago, I've been reminded of the Hikikomori—Japan's estimated 700,000 agoraphobes who, because of their social anxieties, have never escaped their parents' nests.

The shut-ins that are in their forties are called First Generation Hikikomori, and they face what's known as the 2030 Problem. Never having left the house, the dilemma boils down to how they will survive when their parents get old and die.

Drinking coffee in the morning with my dad and my stepmom these mornings, I resemble one of these introverted losers. I have no desire to go out on the streets of Gijón alone. I am perfectly happy at the little table in the spare room, stealing the neighbors Wi-Fi in order to hide away and post this entry.

For those of you joining the blog midstream, my research into human stampedes is taking me to Germany next week, where I will interview survivors of 2010s Love Parade catastrophe, and speak with scientists at the University of Duisburg-Essen about their methodologies for researching its causes and events. After Germany, I'll be headed to India to make observations at the site of the 2008 Chamunda Devi Temple stampede, and to talk with professors from the Indian Institute of Technology about their findings.

For someone like me who can barely leave the house, much less feel comfortable among tens of thousands, the approaching weeks have my apprehension bar pushed up to the maximum. I have returned to my counting exercises to help calm me down, and it's like I'm squirreling away my private time when I get it, because I know it's soon to evaporate.

At least Asturias is less run over by tourists than other parts of Spain, and the bunching and bustle of the crowds in Gijón's downtown is more tolerable than in the hearts of many other Spanish cities.

Actually, at the risk of ruining it, the relative obscurity of this province means Asturias is one of the cooler places to travel in this country. Green and wet and cloudy and Celtic, it's where—contrary to the popular song—the rain truly falls in Spain. The mountain chain running east-west across this part of the geography—the Cordillera Cantabrica—forces the precipitation to drop in the north, leaving the regions to the south with considerably less.

The simulacrums of the pampas in the Sergio Leone movies, the flashy dresses and the moaning crooning of the sweaty Flamenco reproduced worldwide, the ritualized bullfighters—most of the world's stereotypes of Spain—are not products of this region, which identifies itself more with the steady millennia of cold storm clouds coming in off the Bay of Biscay, and the remnants of Pagan cultures, than with the succession of cultural conquests to the south.

In fact, just as the popular vision of the southern United States is tied to slavery and the Civil War, Asturias' identity in the minds of Spaniards is wrapped up with the reconquest of the Iberian Peninsula from the "Moors," and the expulsion of the Jews and gypsies, things that today would be called ethnic cleansing.

The flag of Asturias is a golden cross on a sky-blue field, and every Asturiano knows that it is Pelayo's cross, which appeared to the Visigothic nobleman in a vision, before he led a band of fighters to a "historic" victory against North African armies approaching from regions south into Covadonga, somewhere around the year 718 CE.

If we are to believe the history—which the more I read the more I doubt—a ragtag group, described by the seventeenth century historian Ahmed Mohammed al-Maqqari as "thirty wild donkeys," repelled a significantly larger and better-equipped army, and by doing so terminated the expansion of the Umayyad Caliphate along a line roughly corresponding to the cordillera.

It seems more likely that the so-called Moors were already maxing out their expansionist ambitions, than that the primitive guerrilla groups of Pelayo and his progeny succeeded in any real way militarily, but because a line was believed to have been drawn here in Asturias, the flag of the province might be seen to represent cultural relics of deep racial and ethnic phobias.

Having recently been home in Georgia, the Asturian flag reminds me of that state's flag, and the great hoodwinking that took place with its recent rebranding. The remnants of the Confederate flag that were still present on the Georgia flag were coming under increasing criticism because of the history of slavery that they have been interpreted as representing. In a great backroom sleight of hand that deserves more attention than it received, the state legislature agreed to replace the offensive blue cross, that was technically the Confederate *battle* flag, with the two red stripes and one white stripe of what was the *actual* flag of the Confederacy. Even though it originally stood for the Confederacy more than the one that was removed, the current flag flies high without objections.

But I digress.

As the Iberian Peninsula was increasingly cleared of its Berber and Arab occupiers, Christians across Europe fired up quasi-religious offensives in the Holy Land too. The Crusades just keep swinging back and forth, and now, in 2011, it's like the tenth century all over again, with things getting crazy in Egypt, Libya, and Syria, and whispers of a new caliphate.

When I was improving the focus of my dissertation with Professor Bassoff last year, he recommended that I read Charles Mackay's seminal work *Extraordinary Popular Delusions and the Madness of Crowds*, and while the book doesn't treat crowd crush events directly, it does help illuminate the process by which large groups of people are influenced to make poor choices. Mackay devotes over a hundred pages to the crusades. It was Mackay's opinion that a succession of popes sent the noble fighters of Europe to the Middle East in order to be killed, so that the Church could maintain its control at home.

The other book Bassoff recommended distilled this opinion still further. In Elias Canetti's powerful and puzzling masterpiece, *Crowds and Power*, the author demonstrates that societies tend to send their warriors elsewhere to fight and die with each other in a natural process that serves to purge would-be killers from their home populace. The existing power structure generally stands to benefit from the cycle, and if the process results in a more stable society back home, the wrangling over the justifications for war becomes even more of a moral shitstorm, with each side capable of claiming the high ground on their piles of shit.

Of the two works, Canetti's might be the less famous, but his book stayed with me after reading it—rocked my world really—and while little of it concerns the types of crowd events I'm dealing with in my research, his observations on human behavior are truly profound, often poetic, and at times bordering on the mystical.

Canetti was an Austrian of Sephardic Jewish heritage, and the book's original title in German, *Masse und Macht*, sounds more lyrical than its English translation. I imagine the same holds true for the rest of the book because Canetti was very poetic, and used a poet's language to tackle subjects usually left to social scientists. Currently, I'm not sure if the book has helped me or hurt me, because while it illuminates many of the over-looked causes and correlations of human actions, from the personal to the universal, the same revealing light falls on the myriad monsters that remain unexplainable and impenetrable.

The book begins with a disturbing passage about the fear of being touched, a powerful meditation about our visceral ab-horrence of being in contact with anything that's not us. We have a tendency toward separation that goes back genetically to our earliest attempts at being, when we put up walls to become cells to differentiate ourselves from everything else.

Riding a bus here in Gijón a few days ago, when my personal space was being encroached on all sides and I was slipping into my panic state, trying to control my breathing and doing my counting, it was Canetti's shape-shifting visions that sped through my brain, and they did not pacify my racing heart, my standing suffocation. Instead, the imagery seemed to exacerbate the symptoms. The way he reduces our actions to the animal, to the primitive and the primate, and still further to the most basic, the amoebic, reminds us that our fates are inseparable from our beastly nature, and that we might escape our dire situation as surely as the proverbial pig might fly.

But Canetti's work is full of reversals, and just as surely as we abhor the contact of strangers in certain situations, we abandon all concern and enjoy it in others. Cells differentiate themselves, but they also possess a tendency to come together, and *Crowds and Power* is a thorough and unusual exploration of the human inclination to form and to disband groups, and of the behaviors and traditions that follow from group formation.

"Crowd" is a nebulous concept the way Canetti uses it, consisting of almost any selection of humans that can be set apart or categorized. People riding together on public transportation form what he calls a "mild" crowd, regardless of whether they are conscious of it, and as such they will tend toward collusion despite being composed of unrelated persons.

That's how he describes it early in the book, but further on we see how individuals who become conscious of themselves as separate from the crowd risk sliding into panic, and this is the direction I was heading in the other day. After my exercises failed to calm me down, I gave up and exited the bus the next time the doors opened.

The way Canetti explains it, a crowd's chief characteristic is the desire to increase in size. The individuals within it are not necessarily conscious of the crowd's inclinations—a great example of swarm intelligence, spontaneous order, collective thought, whatever you want to call it. From the agoraphobe's perspective, it's difficult to imagine the crowd being unconscious of itself, but Canetti gives little consideration to the percentage of us that tremble among the multitudes.

The largest crowds, the most obvious and ongoing, are those that arise in opposition to another, the clearest examples being man/woman, and us/them. Canetti calls these double crowds, and in a beautiful twist he proposes that one side does not have to exist, or at least be alive, to constitute a crowd.

Here he's talking about the dead, the unborn, and those who are believed to be in heavens, hells, and limbos, and he argues that all religions begin with our interactions, physical and psychological, with these "invisible" crowds. Thinking like this, these can be the largest crowds imaginable—everybody who has ever existed, or everybody who has yet to, or both.

This is Canetti at his best, when he demonstrates that our mortality sums up a never-ending contest between "two enemies of unequal strength," between the relatively small number of those who currently live, and the necessarily much larger number of those who have already died. Attempting to

elucidate our sorry lot, he writes that it is a "general epidem-
ic of death which confronts us," the type of thought that in
various incarnations is at home in the mind of either an agoraphobe or a person caught up in a human stampede. When
I read the first part of *Crowds and Power*, where it discusses
these unseen assemblies, I realized how prescient Canetti was,
writing in the 1950s. Today, what is Facebook but a collection
of nonexistent collections? A great portion of the world's
internet activity reduces to joining or quitting these invisible
crowds, groups which coalesce around real or imaginary nodes
that Canetti calls "crowd crystals."

I escaped the all-too-real and visible pack of people on the
bus, only to find myself on a sidewalk similarly busy, so I
turned off into an empty alcove and tried to look at anything
but people, trying to act like I wasn't having problems breathing. I stared at indecipherable graffiti tags, curlicued by black
markers on stucco.

Walking helps generally, once I regain my composure, as long
as I can keep moving. The clouds had been threatening all
morning, and they let go while I made my way down Calle
Cabrales. Arriving back at my father's rental, wet and later
than planned, I offered no explanation and told him I really
needed a hot shower.

Since I brought along a digital recorder to interview witnesses
of the Duisburg incident when I get to Germany, I thought it
would be cool to interview my dad while I had it with me, and
later that evening we sat at the kitchen table and got around a
half hour recorded.

Mostly I asked about his life before I knew him: his childhood in Spain, the years in Canada before moving to the States, some time in Miami. My parents divorced when I was ten. There was a stepmother, and then another. I had no questions about those years, I wanted to know how he got to them. But while the facts were forthcoming, the feelings were not.

Without emotion, he relayed the details and dates, and I guess I knew better than to expect sentiments or solicitudes. He is a man who has accomplished things and he's comfortable with just that. He believes in science the way others believe in higher powers, and because everything reduces to physics and facts, sometimes it's like his children are nothing but evidence that he was once incapable of controlling his irrational, animal passions. In his opinion science proves nothing matters or means anything, and perhaps because children are prone to rebel against their parents' positions, I decided early on that science *doesn't* prove nothing matters, but instead sits simply mute on the subject. Meaning must be a language that science, and therefore my father, cannot speak.

I have always understood and accepted his rational atheism, it's his concrete confidence that I'm increasingly bewildered by. Whereas my own supply of self-assurance appears to be atrophying with age, my dad's seems to be fortified by his advancing years. My increasingly agoraphobic tendencies, which apparently are not genetically derived, are something that I have not yet had the courage to discuss with him. But just as I remain close-lipped on certain subjects, there are parts of my father's history that he has yet to divulge.

I know that something formative and formidable happened with a woman named Maria during his youth, but so far all of my attempts to pry open this past have been met with diversion. I asked him about her again for the recording, and he said we could talk about it some other time. Without his answers about this mystery woman I make them up myself. Does he think the things that I'm forced to imagine are better or worse than the truth? Lacking any particulars, the fabricated explanations have got to be more fantastical than the actual, so why does he continue to refrain?

We got into talking about the time he spent studying at the university in Salamanca, and he explained that in the sixteenth century, Francisco de Vitoria and his followers there led a movement toward a reformulation of human rights after the explorations by Columbus and his cohorts. It didn't seem fair that dominion could be asserted over entire continents by monarchs who had recently been unaware of their existence, and de Vitoria's circle was perhaps the first group of Europeans to openly question the legitimacy of the Old World's claims over the New. Similar to Rousseau's concepts of popular sovereignty, the School of Salamanca put forth ideas suggesting that a group of people, or a nation as a whole, is more important than the sum of its parts—concepts that lead logically to the overthrow of despots and unpopular governments. Not surprisingly, here's the emergence thing again.

Proud of Spain's history of liberal philosophy, my father pointed out that the Occupy movement, currently causing a ruckus in various American cities, has its origins in the Indignados movement that got started here in Spain back in

May. The indignant activists set up camp in Madrid's Puerto del Sol and other important city plazas, and created the template for the takeover of Zuccotti Park in Manhattan. I will leave it to my friends with fewer social anxieties to join the tumescent multitudes manifesting.

The weather cleared up the next day, and I ventured downtown with my father to see the several minor tourist attractions Gijón has to offer. First we went to the International Museum of the Gaita, a smallish gallery space exhibiting the Iberian evolution of what most Americans would call a bagpipe.

Apparently the proto-bagpipe came to the peninsula from the Middle East during the later part of the first millennium, and then jumped over the Bay of Biscay to Scotland, where more pipes and frills were added, and its origins were for the most part forgotten or ignored. Although they're proud of holding back the so-called Moorish conquest, the Asturianos have embraced the gaita like no other province, except maybe Galicia, and the instrument is perhaps the best-known representation of the region. No cultural event here is complete without the drone and squeal of the inflated red goatskin. It didn't take long to absorb the displays, and I was quietly happy that it was not a popular museum.

Having grown up here in Gijón, my dad had never paid much attention to the Revillagigedo Palace, which occupies a prime site not far from the Gaita Museum, adjacent to Plaza Mayor and overlooking the port. In a dilapidated state during Dad's youth, its crenelated towers and arched halls have been restored and reopened, and for a few euros you can stroll through it and get a glimpse of what it was like to be rich in Spain in the eighteenth century.

I was surprised to learn that the guy who the palace was built for was none other than Juan Vicente de Güemes Pacheco de Padilla y Horcasitas, segundo conde de Revillagigedo—the second viceroy of New Spain. While the San Juan Islands of Washington State were ostensibly named for Saint John, it's probable that the explorers chose the moniker as a tribute to their viceroy Juan as well. Since I had been living in the San Juans before moving to Seattle for grad school, it seemed like a great, strange, serendipitous discovery.

Juan's time as viceroy came toward the end of Spain's expansionist era, and thoughts about the rights of indigenous peoples to their own sovereignty came to mind again while we toured the salons and antechambers. It must have been a curious thing to be the king's surrogate on a "new" continent, populated almost entirely by peoples of different cultures. Attempts to govern the masses inevitably involved a forced Catholicism. Different forms of compulsory group membership have been one of the hallmarks of our power structures ever since we were monkeys. "Coming together is more important than the sermon," is what Canetti writes in *Crowds and Power*, demonstrating that regular rituals of group cohesion exhaust energies that would otherwise erupt as periodic violence.

Canetti breaks down power to its most basic constituents in a way I had never heard before, illustrating that the most fundamental family unit, mother and child, has within it the blueprint of total tyranny. In complete control of the baby's life and death, the mother holds all the reins of power, and because this dynamic can be inverted easily to demonstrate that the baby is tyrant too, it becomes a great example of Canetti's take on governance and power structures in general.

In many ways power is constructed of commands, which Canetti considers to be threats in their most basic form. He writes that the first command was "a death sentence," and the primordial options were essentially fight or flight, eat or be eaten. A whole fascinating section of the book gets into the forgotten relationships between power structures and the processes of eating, digestion, and even defecation. When one considers certain early African and Polynesian societies where the king was expected to be the fattest individual in the community, the connections between consumption and control solidify. Like with a pride of lions, he who consumes the most is often the most powerful.

There's another great section of Canetti's book that explicates the various traditions in the coronations of nineteenth century West African kings. In these societies the kings were chosen, not inherited, and their reigns were temporary, only lasting for a given period of years—sometimes four, or maybe eight—after which they were killed. He describes these short-term monarchs as cultural indicators of increase or decrease, figureheads upon which to hang the tribe's collective psychic garbage, replaced at intervals to allow for a clean slate. Our current political system in the US retains most of these ancient traditions. Using a contemporary analogy,

President Obama is nothing but a computer's icon for the file "America," picked from the lame choices available with the current operating system, because it's too much of a pain in the ass to upload a different symbol. We'll select another one when we reboot the OS in a few years.

Canetti's book is well known for postulating correlations between paranoia and power, demonstrating that ultimate control is the other side of ultimate fear. The dictator is right next to the schizophrenic on the continuum of crazy, and just as everyone is out to get the paranoiac in his fantasies, those who would remove him truly surround the despot.

Spain's own not-so-distant dictator, Francisco Franco, is an obvious example of a tyrant willing to secure his power by removing those who might protest it, and the evidence of his butchery has popped up in the news again lately, as human rights groups have attempted to unearth the mass graves of Spanish Civil War era political assassinations. In the wake of Franco's death in 1975, his henchmen in the government instituted the Pact of Forgetting, prohibiting the investigation of deaths and disappearances perpetrated during Franco's rule. Legal wrangling over the law's constitutionality has erupted recently as excavations at sites like Piedrafita de Babia have unearthed the undeniable evidence of the Franco regime's atrocities. My father says the *deshuesaderos*—the bone yards—are scattered across the entire country, but that not all of them were filled in by Franco's side.

Canetti writes that "behind all power lies the urge to get others out of the way," and I found this overlaps nicely with my own social phobias and my research on crowd crush. In most life-and-death scenarios, real or imagined, the impulse to persevere overrides all other instincts, and because limitless dead pile up on either side of our brief now, every survivor is a prince of the present, or as Canetti puts it, "each of us is a king in a field of corpses."

But it's a strange type of potentate when you're in the middle of a meltdown. I decided to venture out alone the day after touring the Revillagigedo Palace, and ran into the problems I hinted at in the beginning of the post. Heading east along El Muro, I felt comfortable enough at first, walking fast and avoiding eye contact with the mostly elderly strollers, keeping my attention on the white-capped sea, or on the cement ahead of me, but after a kilometer or so, apprehensions started sneaking in when I stole a few glances at the faces of passersby.

Something about what is traded between eyes—what in ages past was believed to be an actual physical exchange of minuscule particles—something about the visages which I couldn't help but see as disapproving caused the air to feel suddenly short of oxygen, my breaths no longer feeling sufficient to aerate my blood, my head shrinking inside like one balloon deflating inside another. All these faulty facets combined to force me to the border of breakdown by the time I reached the La Loca statue.

Patinated brass, about five meters tall, forever looking north over the Mar Cantabrico, the Monument to the Mother of the Immigrant stands distraught and windblown, one arm outstretched, pointing to an absence, forlorn.

Installed in 1970, the sculpture was created by Ramón Muriedas as a memorial to all the heartaches, and broken families, and split histories that are the result of world immigration. But because of the figure's distressed countenance, the locals call her La Loca—The Crazy.

There were a few tourists taking pictures when I walked up to the towering maniac, and I guess it was their glances and cameras that threw me over the edge. A rush hit me, and I looked out toward the sea, and it turned into flames, thousands of gleamings spreading suddenly from one. It was a tide of light, I turned away confused, and the buildings in the distance transformed into a forest. Like my episode at Montserrat, this panic attack was accompanied by hallucinations, except this time they were far more elaborate and vivid.

Within a crowd all the strings are gone. Say goodbye to the boundaries, the borders, the stings. Outside the cactus of torment, you step from yourself to a place where whatever you eat consumes you. The beaming faces, the smiling joyful faces, become covered in dust and veiled in darkness. Like the image of reaped corn, there is equity before death.

A flock of birds shimmered and turned into a rain of coins, then the coins became bottles, then the vision doubled itself. Creeping creatures left the ground and whirled through the air with the wind. Golden-winged spiders cavorted above bumbling beetles and bugs. Incipient snakes and vermin grew to rats, then gendarmes, then enemy horsemen, and singular

bogeymen, some on stilts. Monstrous abortions and manne-
quins, devils, fire rowdies, fleas. Laughing painted girls, ants
and toads, a web of delicate threads disappearing like quicksil-
ver, and the cracks became needles, and secret doors hidden
in the ground. It tripled, then it quadrupled, and La Loca
became a creature dancing, with fifty heads and a hundred
legs and arms.

A voice whispered, "You are the heap of shit at the center of
the universe."

First we are seized, then cut up, then consumed and assimi-
lated. Corrosives and constricting pressures are applied during
the long, winding trip to the asshole, a considerable supply
of neurons assist the process, then we are birthed into a pile,
loaded with blood guilt, the compressed sum of the evidence
of murder, the stink of our daily sins crying out. We are most
alone with our excrement. We can only be alone with our shit.
Without it the powers are hidden. It is the very proof of our
everything.

I staggered toward the ocean, climbed over the low wall that
separated the paved area from the rocky drops to the water,
and I hid from the visions inside a recess of stone.

Today, I've stayed in again and composed this blog post.

Sending.

PARIS

October 1, 2011

2005 Baghdad Stampede

2010 Phnom Penh Stampede

catacombs   complex system failures

compressive asphyxiation   crowd crush categories

crowd disintegration   mass panic vs. mass hysteria

Occupy   sewer tour

The train out of Gijón was an ancient Talgo, an aging example of the world's first articulated carriages, capable of leaning into curves to improve stability. First rolled out in the 1940s, they are heavy and wide, and this one retained one of the original color schemes. Almost everything was Guardia Civil green inside. Knowing the trains debuted to international acclaim, older Spaniards like my father are still proud of them, and once, on a Talgo near Madrid, I was scolded by a wrinkled abuela for putting my feet up on the recently reupholstered seat cushion across from me.

Sometimes practicality means going south in order to go north again, so instead of taking local trains through Cantabria and the Basque region, I headed backward to Burgos, where I took a more direct train to Paris. It was one of the ubiquitous Talgo IIIs, with a thick red stripe down the exterior, and ocean-green accents inside. Is it okay if I prefer to focus on the trains instead of my mental condition?

Because I have friends from Washington State living in Paris, I had a great opportunity to tour the city for a few days before continuing to my research in Duisburg, so I picked up a guidebook in Gijón, and made methodical work of it while the sunflower fields of southern France flew by outside.

The crowd on the train was okay, but I had worries about exiting into the hustle of the Gare d'Austerlitz and the metro, so I upped my dose of tranquilizers while the ugly sprawl of the city's suburbs passed the window. By the time I stepped down from the train I had entered the semi-catatonic zone from which few details are retrieved, although I do recall how slow the Paris subway seemed to crawl. The stops were so close together that at several stations I could see people waiting at the next station down the tunnel, and even in an anesthetized condition I felt like I could walk faster.

Upon my arrival at Matt and Wendy's flat in the 11th arrondisse-ment, I apologized for my subdued state, blaming a late night and traveling with little sleep, and they set me up with a shower and some dinner. They had been my neighbors on Orcas Island for several years, before Wendy moved the family here so she could attend culinary school, and it was comforting to see famil-iar faces speaking English. Wendy and the kids had school the next day so Matt and I planned what we might get up to.

Matt, originally from Britain, wasn't fond of France, or the French, and he had seen next to none of the city's attractions. He said he'd be happy to join me wherever I might like to go, and when I flipped through the guidebook again I realized there were only two things I had highlighted. Both of them were underground. Matt said he'd be happy to start with the sewers.

In the morning we made our way to the small entrance kiosk bordering the busy Quai d'Orsay, just a stone's throw from the Pont de l'Alma, and the River Seine, and Matt said he couldn't remember who, but somebody famous said that a culture's height is best measured by the sophistication of their waste removal systems.

The smell was not overwhelming as we headed down the stairs, but it's there, and while not unbearably foul it is not pleas-ant. Its chief accent was that of moisture itself, and as the entrance tunnel opened into the first great hall, we entered a light mist, thrown up by the frothy, fast-moving river of excreta that was but one tributary in the complex, Styxian watershed running below old Paris.

The walls were of red brick and plaster while the floors were cement, and the main architectural theme was the arch. Like an underground Alhambra it was shady and cool, but filled by the roar of the rushing waste. Modern metal pipes of various diameters snaked across the ceilings and walls, and upstream progressively smaller tubes fed into the main channel, each echoing the shape of its parents.

The maze was not over-illuminated, which preserved an antique ambiance, and we couldn't help but laugh at how close we could get to the raw sewage. Leaning over one thin chain, I could fully appreciate the channel's depth, its speed, the more subtle of the mist's odiferous accents, and the raw power of gravity in the process of evacuating the city's shit. Individual items surfaced in the bubbles: tampon applicators, wet wipes, particularly solid lumps of feces that had survived the tumbling thus far.

An unsupervised child might easily disappear into the turbulent gulch, and the dangers of the drop reminded me of situations usually found at majestic park overlooks in wild, remote places, not hidden beneath the centers of upscale urban areas. We read the English translations on some of the informational displays, and looked at early photographs of people getting boat tours of the facilities in the late 1800s.

There's a gift shop, and Matt bought me a blue baseball cap from a selection of official Paris sewer-worker apparel, the slogan *Visite des Égous de Paris* and the city's skyline were laminated across its brow.

We returned to street level and walked a few kilometers south on the Boulevard Raspail to get to our next underground destination. Along the way Matt said it would be hard to top "all that French shit."

One of the most amazing things about the catacombs of Paris is their unobtrusive entrance. I can only imagine that the same venue in the US would be overstated and obnoxious.

How classy of the French to maintain it with a discreet doorway and a small sign. It's death we're dealing with after all.
Perhaps it's better to speak quietly.

A curt gentleman took our euros, and a staircase spiraled us
down one hundred thirty steps below the 14th arrondisse-
ment, to where the dead of early Paris were redeposited after
their graveyards were dug up, facilitating the city's expansion.
The halls had already been hollowed out for their limestone,
and were waiting empty when the municipality decided to
have them filled in again with centuries of accumulated human remains.

We walked through a dim tunnel for a minute before getting to the warning chiseled into stone above an entryway:
"ARRÊTE! C'EST ICI L'EMPIRE DE LA MORT." Going
under it we passed into the galleries of the expired.

When we came to the first alcove, Matt said he was forced
to wonder what difference it makes if you build over the dead
without first reburying and reconsecrating their bones.

He said, "Why is it okay to live above the skeletons once all
their parts have been jumbled with a thousand others, and a
little plaque has been placed with a priest's prayer?"

I suggested that perhaps it was as much a matter of convenience as it was a ritual performed for ghosts. Since otherwise
the dead would continue to pop up incidentally and indefinite-
ly, why not deal with them all at once?

It appeared that they must have packed them to the ceiling, but that several centuries of settling had left a hand-sized gap which allowed us to glimpse above the bones all the way to the back of their crypts. They stowed them efficiently, with walls made of neatly stacked femurs and skulls serving to close up the rooms, and while there are other catacombs in the world, none compare to the volumes, the quantity, and the compactness of these. It's the remains of an estimated six million people cached beneath a small neighborhood.

These rooms must approach the maximum density at which humans could be brought together without burning and/or pulverizing them—way beyond what my crowd density software is designed to measure. My program analyzes data based on digital photos of standing assemblies, and maxes out at nine people per square meter, even though a crush incident is already underway around six or seven ppm². When the crowd is no longer upright my software can't recognize human figures anymore, but there's no use for preventative monitoring once the crowd is piling up vertically.

I said it reminds me of so many classical representations of Hell, where the skeletal masses burning in perpetuity are packed in the flames like screaming sardines.

"The worst part always seemed to me to be the other people, more than the fire," Matt said, in accord with my own sentiments. With scripted timing a loud group of American teenagers passed us. They shrieked and made a big deal about the bones, but Matt and I weren't the slightest perturbed by the death around us. We enjoyed it, really.

I reminded him that Sartre wrote that Hell is other people, and Matt said, "Who?"

It's true though, the classical canvases frequently depict Hell in images that resemble crowd crush, with the congregations crammed together in tableaux exceeding six ppm^2.

After I explained that my crowd density analyzer works equally well on many paintings, he asked me why I was "so into the whole mass panic thing?"

Firstly I made sure he understood the correct nomenclature. Mass panic, or mass hysteria—sometimes called collective delusional behavior—is characterized by illness or delusions spreading through a population, and is categorized separately from crowd crush. The Salem witch trials present a solid example of mass panic, the way things are currently classified.

Matt said he's pretty sure the word panic comes from the god Pan, something I hadn't considered yet.

Crowd crush, the subject I've been studying, has been more commonly known as human stampede phenomenon, but because large fatality incidents rarely resemble a fast moving herd, the word stampede is less and less in favor. In reality, many mass fatality events happen slowly, and the ones that do occur quickly, like fires in theaters, are usually characterized by blocked passageways, where the crowd is never given the opportunity to run wild en masse.

Incidents of crowd crush have been shown to fall into three

categories. Those that are caused by interruptions in normal traffic are perhaps the most common, including accidents at sporting events, concerts, religious festivals, and pilgrimages. Those caused by attempts to escape real or perceived danger are known as flight response, or escape panic, and usually include either a war zone or a disaster, be it manmade or natural. Those caused by the distribution of food, money, or other items are called crazes, and while they happen frequently, they tend to have lower ceilings on their fatality counts.

It isn't a precise vocabulary. Sometimes there are mixed elements, like when you've got a pilgrimage in a war zone. Baghdad in 2005 is a perfect example.

Matt asked what happened there, so I explained. The sector was hot, American troops controlled the city, and they had barricaded one end of the Al-Aaimmah Bridge across the Tigris River. Mortars had already exploded along the pilgrimage route in the morning, killing seven, and injuring dozens, so when someone thought somebody was a suicide bomber later that day near the bridge, the crowd had a low flash point. People choosing the bridge as an escape had no idea they were running into a trap that would prove to be at least several orders of magnitude more fatal than the average suicide bomber. As I mentioned in my post from Barcelona, almost a thousand died on and around the Al-Aaimmah Bridge, perhaps the single deadliest event during the war in Iraq, and it barely made the news back in the States.

Matt touched the ceiling where water dripped from a tiny stalactite.

"But what really happened?" he asked. "How do that many people die that way?"

I proposed we look at it before, during, and after.

It is well understood within the research community that preventative measures are the best way to avoid crowd crush incidents. Both anticipating the future, and dealing with potential mishaps before they manifest are crucial when assembling large numbers of humans, and while seeing what's to come isn't always possible, any attempts to prepare for difficult groups beforehand will have high, if invisible, returns.

Because blog entries are published on top of their predecessors, and often read out of order, perhaps you have already seen into my future by reading the posts I haven't written yet. Maybe you already know what I cannot yet know. But again I digress.

As you head into the venue, or join the procession, it's easy to observe if safety systems are in place to accommodate problems. Are there designated ingress and egress routes? Are there communication systems, like overhead speakers, and walkie-talkies for employees? Are there signs giving clear directions, and are there obvious obstructions or bottlenecks? If it's a large event, are there people or cameras monitoring the situation? Crowd managers should be in place in any event with more than five hundred participants, so do you observe personnel observing you? Are people in the crowd already touching you on all sides? If so, this is a serious warning sign, and density has already reached at least 4ppm^2.

Before the event, volumes are usually lower as people are still arriving, and this is a good time to size up the situation. If things get tight, which way are you going to get out? Sometimes the best answer is the one everyone else *isn't* going to choose. Before the event is the best time to think about it.

John J. Fruin, a leader in the field of crowd studies, and the author of *The Causes and Prevention of Crowd Disasters*, maintains that the cheapest and most effective precautionary measures involve communication, including everything from information received by attendees during the ticketing process, to comments made by performers on stage. Most crush incidents involve an inability of people deep within an assembly to communicate with people farther back. Attempts by security to manipulate the masses from the perimeter don't work very well, and often indicate the game is already lost. The adage that has evolved in the industry says that good crowd *management* means not having to exercise crowd *control*.

I explained to Matt how I'd watched recent videos of the Occupy movement protests, and I'd been impressed by the human microphone phenomenon, and its potential for use in crowd crush situations. One person screams "Mic check!" and then everyone around echoes "Mic check!" in return. Whatever the speaker yells afterward gets repeated in chorus so those farther away can hear the message. With front-to-back communication being so crucial during crushes, the spread of this simple and effective technique promises to save lives if its use can be popularized internationally.

But let's return to the crowd crush. Now you're inside the venue—let's say it's a rock concert—and you're near the front of the audience. As it often happens, they've allowed too many people onto the floor and you're losing your ability to move freely. The revelers are rowdy, and everyone's trying to get closer to the stage. Most Americans have some familiarity with this environment—too many people on a plane, and a number of barriers to their movement. Perhaps people you don't know are getting shoved up against you, as waves of kinetic energy pass through the crowd. These waves have been demonstrated to be good indicators of crowd volume, and there's software being developed that detects them on video, yet another tool that might save lives in the future.

Often the problem area is where the crowd meets the stage—where the front ranks can go no further, and the press from behind puts bodies up against fences or walls. Most of us can think of famous examples of concerts gone wrong. Nine people died in a crush at the 1999 Roskilde Festival during Pearl Jam's performance, so the event holds the dubious distinction of being the last crowd crush incident of the twentieth century. Matt mentioned the notorious The Who concert in 1979. I explained that one involved people crushed outside, against the closed stadium doors during soundcheck, and that rock concerts themselves remain relatively low casualty events, probably because the performers onstage are able to see what is happening, and the PA system allows effective communication with the crowd.

It's the processes of entrance and exit to the concerts that are far more problematic, when heavy crowds come up against bottlenecks or barriers outside the view and the control of supervisory personnel. The obstruction can be a staircase or a hallway, a tunnel, or an overpass, any constriction or drop-off, or even just a corner. Temporary fences or barricades used to direct traffic often become seriously dangerous when they fail under the tremendous forces of a crowd.

In India, where the temples are often atop hills, you get the combination of large crowds, steep grades, and less robust event management, and so higher fatality incidents are more common. Underbuilt railings give way, or slippery terrain causes whole sections of a crowd to fall onto others. It happens so often that they're called temple crushes in India.

But back to being in it. If you're still able to change your position in the crowd, you'll probably find it easier to make headway by attempting movement sideways or diagonally, not forward or backward. One guy that blogs about raves described it as "Left and Right Arrow keys" as opposed to the "Bring All to Front" function.

But imagine it's too late. You didn't get out in time because you weren't really sure which way to go, and now things are getting really tight and you've become part of the mass. At this point we're talking around $7ppm^2$, and you'll be taken wherever the mob takes you. If it gets really bad you come off the ground when the surges come through. Frequently people lose their shoes, but clothes might follow, and there is no way to retrieve them. Those that fall down will find it extremely difficult to get up again. You feel out of balance because you are. Your body's constant micro-adjustments that maintain equilibrium are impossible, and the bodies surrounding you both support and undermine. You might consider it an interesting place to contemplate the existence of free will.

The simple solution seems so obvious, everybody needs to just spread out and stop pushing forward, but Murphy's at war with Occam, and anything that can go wrong just might make a joke out of the most elegant answer to a problem. Take a look at the recent Deepwater Horizon disaster to see a great example of the adage, "complex systems fail in complex ways."

While it may be useful to describe crowd motions in terms of fluid dynamics, the comparison has also been made recently to the behaviors of non-Newtonian fluids, which harden into solids temporarily when exposed to certain pressures or catalysts. Like the chemicals pumped into the ground during hydraulic fracking, a tight crowd can crystallize in an instant, and if you're the one up against the wall or rail when a shockwave sweeps by, it might mean a concussion or broken ribs, or it might mean you crumple to the ground and never make it up again.

Often it's a slow compression, increasing in force incrementally until people start passing out upright. Everyone pushing against you makes it hard to breathe, and the heat alone can be enough to make you faint. If you lose consciousness you might be passed overhead for attempts at resuscitation outside the crush zone, but this will probably only happen in upright crowds that are more or less stationary. Once people start going down in moving, panicked crowds, it's a whole different deal, and when people begin clambering over others to save themselves, it's a horror of an even larger magnitude.

Many times a section of crowd goes down all at once, and those pressing from further back press harder, interpreting the sudden pressure drop as forward progress, like some barrier has finally been removed. Instead the situation has just become a worst-case scenario. This grave misconception has killed countless thousands. So much for the so-called wisdom of the crowd.

Elias Canetti's book *Crowds and Power* contains a gruesome account written by Robert Curzon, a survivor of a crowd crush incident at the Chapel of the Sepulchre in Jerusalem in 1834. Curzon describes making his way past bodies which at first he assumed were resting, until coming upon them in heaps and realizing they were all dead. His descriptions are too gruesome to repeat.

After witnessing this carnage he gets sucked into the melee himself, barely surviving. At one point he was forced to trod upon dead bodies himself, and afterward, he saw hundreds of corpses in heaps head high.

This is the only section of Canetti's book that looks at crowd crush directly, but he touches on the psychology of crush incidents when discussing panics in theaters, during what he calls crowd disintegration. Before the fire, or bomb, or earth-quake, the people in the venue enjoy the unity of the group, together in a common ritual, but when the audience turns into impediment, the solidarity dissolves immediately. And

Canetti explains that the disintegration becomes more violent the more the setting is sealed off.

Now you come to the moral quandary of whether to climb over, or on top of others to save yourself. For some the question is unthinkable, and for others it's not even a question. Between them are most of us.

I understand that it's difficult for Matt to imagine getting crushed, because he's a good candidate for survival. Athletic and lean, he is probably one of those who would climb out, and would probably help to save others once he's escaped, and this brings us to one of the harshest realities: that the fittest and strongest and most savage are better equipped to fight their way out, and it is often the men over the women.

But even the strong go down. Available online there's an interview with Raul Vargas, who was a young man when he survived the Station Nightclub Fire in Rhode Island in 2003. Given a chance to get out, he would have been a candidate for escape, but he wasn't given any. The heap took him by surprise, and then he was beneath it. His account is the most harrowing I've heard, because the people above him burned and died while their bodies insulated him from the tremendous heat.

Vargas had learned as a wrestler that the human rib cage resists compression better if you are on your side, so he created a small pocket to breathe with his arms in front of his face, and lived through it miraculously, one shoulder against the floor. The firemen didn't expect to find anyone still alive while they removed body after body from on top of him.

When the panic subsides, when the fire's out, when the masses have dispersed, what's left is often a tangled pile of corpses that might take hours to unravel. It is more difficult to separate the dead than most people can imagine. The process can completely traumatize the first responders.

When I said it's enigmatic that what happens so fast can take so long to undo, Matt joked that it reminds him of the on-again-off-again separation he's going through with his wife.

"Relationships start out so easy and fun, and then they're so hard to get out of," he said.

Considering what happened to me a few weeks before, I replied that sometimes the actual breakup borders on effort-less, but the feelings in the wake of it are difficult to extricate yourself from. I've gotten through most of two blog posts now without talking about my own recent split, and while I wrote that I wouldn't be mentioning her again anytime soon, I'm not sure it's realistic. Besides, who's to say I'm not just going back and editing her out of my posts? Risking complete honesty, it is eating me inside out.

Anyway, compressive asphyxiation is usually the cause of death, a result of large horizontal forces in upright crowds, or the weight of vertically stacked bodies in crowds that have become heaps. Sometimes the cause of death is what's called traumatic rhabdomyolysis, precipitated by the sudden removal of people from on top of victims being compressed. Also known as crush syndrome, it results in a quick flush of toxins into the bloodstream from tissues that were breaking down without proper circulation. When flow is restored, the kidneys are overloaded with more poisons than they can handle. Someone with steady vital signs can crash and die within minutes once they're "rescued."

Bringing it back around to Baghdad, put the crowd on a closed bridge high above the river, and add the extreme temperatures of August, and you might start to understand why scores of people died. Many passed out because of the heat. Their bodies' cooling systems were overwhelmed in the press of hot flesh. Others jumped or fell from the bridge and subsequently drowned.

What happened in Baghdad is very similar to the incident in Phnom Penh, at the Khmer festival celebrating the temporary reversal of the Tonlé Sap River during the autumnal tidal bore. Although the bridge wasn't closed, it became blocked nonetheless when people lost their balance, and wiring for lighting on the bridge was ripped down in the madness, electrocuting some, increasing the panic, and sending more over the rail into the river.

Thinking about so many dead in the water, it's of note that the word *emergency* derives from *emergence*, which breaks down in Latin to *ex+mergere*. To come out of the water. Essentially the opposite of *submerge*.

I explained to Matt that it's sort of unbelievable there's no footage of the Baghdad tragedy in 2005. Just five years later, many pieces of the Phnom Penh event were captured on video, and the Duisburg incident the same year was so rich in various electronic data that it is the first crush event to be analyzed in detail using electronic mapping, locational awareness, and GPS technologies.

Thankfully Duisburg also proved what researchers had already conjectured, that humanity is not completely lost during these tragedies. Caught on video are numerous instances of assistance and cooperation, and for every guy climbing over hapless innocents, there's another who lends a hand.

By this point in our conversation, Matt and I had wandered our way over to the exit stairs, so we headed up. After a cursory check by an employee to make sure we weren't stealing anyone's bones, we came back out into the noise and bustle of the Rue Rémy Dumoncel, about six blocks away from the catacomb's entrance. Annoyed by the real world again, Matt said he preferred it underground where it's cool and quiet, and I laughed with him, agreeing completely.

We got back to his place, swilled some wine, and had dinner with Wendy and the kids. Matt kept thanking me for the tour, saying it was the best day he'd had in France so far.

I had their flat to myself this morning and was free to compose this post.

Sending.

DUISBURG

October 5, 2011

2010 Love Parade Disaster   crowd collapse

das unheimliches   high speed rail

Life in a Day   massenpanik

mirror matter   mirror neurons

Rhine-Ruhr   sousveillance

The red wedge of the electric engine on the Thalys train gave a speedy impression, even when parked motionless like it was when I arrived at Gare du Nord for the four hour trip to Duisburg. Abstract white streaks swept back from the nose, and one of them outlined a woman's profile, with hair flowing behind her in the imagined wind. The carriages that came after were mostly the silver of unpainted aluminum alloy, with a thick, red stripe across the top, above the windows, tying them all together.

I was early, and the crowd density inside the antique station sent me outside again to kill time before boarding. With 700,000 passengers per day, Gare du Nord is one of the busiest train stations in the world, and even though the streets

and sidewalks that adjoin it don't offer much of a reduction
in hustle and bustle, I felt better once I escaped the massive,
chaotic, echoing hall. At 55,000 people per square mile, Paris
itself ranks in the world's top twenty most densely populated
municipalities, and I was happy to be heading to more sparsely
occupied places—at least until I got to Mumbai.

Hungry for a snack, I sat down at a café across the street and
admired the great, windowed arch of the station's exterior,
crowned by statues of various personas representing European
cities, and punctuated in the center with a clock. Several
young couples nearby were obviously in love, and I was immediately jealous of them, wondering if I would ever get the
chance to be one of them, to share croissants and café au laits
with a sweetheart on the sidewalks of Paris. But perhaps in a
blog post it's better to mimic what they call lossy data compression, and discard some of my extraneous personal information, so that the bits are organized and stored more efficiently.

Inside the Thalys, the upholstery was all red, and everything
else was white, and the seats were assigned like on an airplane.
The man sitting next to me was well tailored and appeared
more or less conservative. From what little I heard him say, I
think he was probably German. It seemed to be the predominant language onboard.

In that section of the train the seats were aligned in rows that
faced each other, and mine faced backwards. As we left the
station I hoped that the train might be reoriented outside
the terminus, but after fifteen minutes of watching Paris
disappear retrograde, I tried to settle into the uncomfortable

opposite perspective. Instead of seeing Germany coming at me, I saw France and Belgium rushing away.

I was scheduled to tour the site of the 2010 Love Parade crowd crush incident the next day, to take measurements and share observations, so I tried to organize the topics of discussion I was to have with Professors Boehm and Lutz from the University of Duisburg-Essen, and I brushed up on my German. I wanted to make sure and know the translations of the most basic relevant terminology, like *Massenpanik* and *Ausstieg*, but the landscape pulling away from me outside the window got me out of balance, and made it hard to focus. I stumbled upon the word *torschlusspanik*, which translates to "gate shut panic" in English. The fear of running out of time.

As the train got up to high speed, its kinetic energy translated through the environment and it was no longer so easy to move in the aisle. When I stood up to go to the bathroom, everything was jerky. Our larger vector managed our mass, and I felt forces from the small adjustments in the carriage multiplied in my body. I remembered watching videos of high-speed rail disasters and considered their obvious similarities to airplane accidents. A train wreck at over two-hundred miles per hour resembles a plane crash, minus the fireball, and the bright yellows of the flotation devices and oxygen masks scattered in the aftermath.

As we exited France, we entered what some people call the Blue Banana, the enormous area of urbanization and manufacturing that bends south from the Liverpool and Manchester region, through Holland, and Belgium, through the middle of Germany to Switzerland, and northern Italy. Within this huge geographic boomerang churns the world's greatest assemblage of wealth and industry. Seen from space, the curve glows almost solid white with lights at night, and the banana shape is blue when depicted on maps, to reflect the color of the European Union's flags and logos.

The train stopped in Liege, and then Aachen, then Cologne, where our route turned north again and began to follow the Rhine River. Flowing all the way from its origin in the Swiss Alps to the divided delta around Rotterdam, the Rhine once demarcated the limits of the Roman Empire, and today the river would be the banana's spine, if bananas had spines.

We entered Germany's Rhine-Ruhr metropolitan area, the largest conurbation in Europe, a polycentric megacity of eleven million people that mushroomed during the Industrial Revolution out of easily extractable coal deposits and convenient river trans-portation. They call it the land *von kohle und stahl*—of coal and steel—and it is the backbone of the country's *wirtschaftswunder*, the busiest industrial region on the Continent.

In 2010, it was Rhine-Ruhr's turn to be one of the European Capitals of Culture, and this led to the itinerant Love Parade music festival being staged in Duisburg. It was the first time the Capital of Culture award had been given to a region instead of a city, but as the region is sort of like one big city, they tweaked the rules a little.

In Cologne, the men across from me, too similar to myself to be remarkable, were replaced by a mother and daughter. The little girl was wearing a lion costume, and she swung her legs excitedly and played with her pin-on tail. She kept looking at me, but her mother didn't.

Then it happened again.

The future is a train. The panic attack is a train, granted preordainment by the rails on which it rides, unstoppable, right on schedule even.

If we live in a quantum reality it means the particle knows ahead of time about the slit—about the shit—it will pass through. And why wouldn't it?

I knew this would happen.

Look at the time-control buttons on our keyboards and screens. The past is on the left, and the future is on the right, and proceed is a triangle that points from the one to the other, not from the other to the one.

It usually starts with feeling the blood moving in my veins, and different areas seem to circulate at different speeds and volumes. It races through my fingers, my ears, my scalp, and goes sluggish in my legs and gut. A thermodynamic kaleidoscope of various pressures mixes inside me until I feel like a breathing fractal. A bleeding, spiraled tie-dye of flesh. Eventually I will overfocus on the fluid rushing through my heart, the scary cynosure of the elevated pulse and uncontrolled respiration. The pumping paranoiac knot.

It helps sometimes to multiply imaginary numbers on a mental blackboard, focusing on the simple processes of abstract arithmetic instead of the real world whirlpools dizzying me, but as often as not the exercise does nothing to hold back the slide into the blurred reality. The beforemath slips into the during, the discordance with my self.

Ausflippen, ängstlichkeit, austasten.

I get *das unheimliches.* One thing can't be both here and there. It's like my psyche is a misunderstanding, or simply imaginary, and there is no I. My ego is nothing, a make-believe master of disparate data. Merely the dot that indicates my current location.

The multiplication didn't work.

The little girl could tell I was freaking out.

This is where thoughts become physical, as each one ratchets on the previous in an incremental asphyxia. They aren't things that can be described, but figments and phantoms, fragments of the rational. Traces of ideas with strong chemical signatures, capable of catastrophic internalized sea changes.

I avoided looking at the man sitting next to me. I'm pretty sure only the lion girl could tell I was in the middle of my own little Fukushima.

And every time it happens I ask myself, will this one be my final break with reality? Will this mark the beginning of the next completely fictional me? While the changes consume me so easily, I'm convinced they won't just wash away like a flood.

This time I thought of Canetti's writing on crowds, about how fear was capable of becoming its reverse, and I wondered if I could turn the emotions around. What's the opposite of a panic attack? A flush of supreme confidence? The feeling of invincibility that's only possible when you're the sole survivor amid the corpses of your enemies, or the debris of a train wreck? Perhaps the emotions present when killing or torturing someone would be the flip side of utter anxiety. Total satisfaction and confidence while in control of someone else's horror and fate. I failed to muster anything that resembled the inverse of my fears.

The freak-out thoughts were wrong-way and de-thinking. Unrememorable. Nothing about them constituted a narrative.

There were three stops for Dusseldorf, and I was kind of getting my mostly invisible shit under control when we departed for the third time. The girl returned to her pin-on tail and stared out the window instead of at me, and the train rolled at a much less catastrophic speed.

Arriving in Duisburg by rail is unspectacular, unless you're a fan of industrialization and its accessories. Warehouses and railway yards filled up the flat landscape, and graffiti might have been the prettiest thing to look at. A majority of the region's blast furnaces were in Duisburg during WWII, and one of the largest inland ports in the world was just upriver, two facts that led to more bombs being dropped on Duisburg during the war than any other Axis city.

It was a short walk from the train station south to the plain, red-brick box that was the Hotel Ibis Duisburg Hauptbahnhof, and even though the population density here is only about 5,400 people per square mile—and only about half a million residents—I didn't mess around getting to the quiet of my room. Outside, I noticed that the city's flag was a black, double-headed eagle on yellow, above a white castle on red. I checked in. After taking some sleeping pills, I re-watched various YouTube videos of the Love Parade disaster, and then I passed out on the über-modern sofa.

The next morning I met with Boehm and Lutz from the University of Duisburg-Essen at a café next to campus. I made sure to be sufficiently sedated, and apologized for seeming tired.

Boehm was older than I expected, with hair fully white, and Lutz looked like a young Hedy Lamarr without all the make-up. Both of them were really excited about a new study on the Love Parade incident published by Dirk Helbing of the Germany Academy of Sciences. Helbing is like a god among crowd crush researchers. His early work modeling self-driven, many-particle systems is considered seminal, and his "Slower is faster" aphorism is known throughout the field. Borrowing well-understood equations from the mechanics of grain hoppers and funnels, Helbing added numbers for what he called "repulsive interaction force," which is the tendency of people in a crowd to not want to touch each other, and for "interpersonal friction," to represent the tendency of people to get stuck together too.

He also succeeded in getting usable computer simulations of human movement patterns, and one of the cooler things to come out of this early research was the discovery that optimal survival numbers in an escape situation come from a combination of individualistic *and* herd behavior. "Everyone for themselves" is not necessarily better than "we're all in it together."

Helbing is head of a project trying to win a billion-euro grant for a linked supercomputer network that will have the power to predict events such as world financial crises; a digital crystal ball into the future, crunching torrential data and un-understandable algorithms. I'm forced to wonder if he's thought about applying his own "slower is faster" concept to the reality of his current project. By trying to cheat the future could he be slowing down the now?

His paper that's coming out soon in cooperation with Pratik Mukerji, explicates the numerous variables that cascaded to produce the 2010 Love Parade catastrophe. It's a holistic approach to the event's causality, and I was surprised to hear it includes an event scale similar to the one I'm designing, except that theirs goes from zero to eight, while mine involves two elements. One through five for volume, and A through E for topography.

Helbing and Mukerji have introduced an interesting new term, *crowd quake*, to better describe a Love Parade type of event, but Boehm and Lutz say the coolest new term they've heard tossed around is *crowd collapse*, because it better describes the domino effect that sweeps through some crowd zones in many fatal incidents.

Boehm and Lutz are friends with Barbara Krausz, who has the new software to detect the subtle waves that roll from one side to another in assemblies, indicating what has been dubbed *crowd sway*. Video cameras linked to networked daemons can easily observe shifts in pixel fields, indicating the types of turbulence that cause fatalities. They say it shows great promise.

Talk about density led us into talking about Lutz's impressive new work that looks at the effects of smartphone use on crowd behavior. Because operating phones in tight crowds requires more personal space, their pervasive usage might help reduce initial crowd densities, and so far her numbers seem to corroborate the theory. She got visibly excited when I told her about the application I've proposed to estimate crowd densities via phone.

We hopped in Lutz's ancient Audi and went south on Autobahn 59, chatting about the Love Parade investigations and prosecutions moving through various government agencies. It's been over a year since the tragedy, but the locals are still understandably upset about it.

Boehm got fired up talking about regressive research programs. She said that people who study research processes, who scrutinize the techniques of inquiries and their outcomes, can now detect the presence of a cover-up or conspiracy based on the results of the inquiries. If the official story generates more closed doors than positive or negative facts when compared with independent inquiries—facts which themselves can lead to more facts—then it indicates a regressive program, essentially a cover-up.

I said, "You mean like the 9/11 Commission Report?," and she gave me a dismissive "Duh."

She said the Helbing paper on the Love Parade is very careful not to point fingers, even though it's clear the event never should have been permitted.

"It was canceled in previous years because of the very obvious problems with the size of the festival," she said.

Lutz chimed in, "There's just too much love to put in one place."

We exited the highway at Mercatorstraße, and pulled over in a gravelly area adjoining an empty industrial lot. They call it brownfield here, the post-industrialized spaces and parks, and Duisburg has plenty of it. The site they chose for the Love Parade used to be a rail yard, with Autobahn 59 and Böninger Park to the west, and another active rail yard to the east. The curious reader might gather other details from Google Maps.

The entrance for the event, which was the ramp on Karl-Lehr Street, wasn't large enough to handle the human traffic. As several obstructions had been placed on the ramp, including a shipping container and several police cordons, and since the ingress was also functioning as the egress, there was no way the ramp could pass the recommended people-per-square-meter-per-minute minimum. Compounding this was a late start, causing the crowds to build up outside the venue, and then overwhelm the entry area once they were allowed in.

We donned neon-green safety vests and started out across the grass and dirt that had been the main festival area, where the stage had been set up.

The day of the Love Parade catastrophe also happened to be the exact date that hundreds of amatuer and professional filmmakers around the world were shooting footage of their lives to be compiled into a feature-length movie called *Life in a Day*. Several individuals were taking video of their experiences at the Love Parade to be submitted to the *Life in a Day* project, and significant footage ended up in the film. Starting at the time stamp 1:20:32, about two and a half minutes are given to the festival, and the footage gives a good impression of what the event was like.

Initially you can see the music floats, the colorful decorations, the smiles on faces, the revelers in funny clothes, the DJs spinning before the masses, and you can hear the techno music, and the jubilant sounds of the crowds. But then you hear sirens, and the music goes dark, and you see people's uncertain faces as they are stuck in giant, unmoving mobs. The documentary has no narration and no useful footage of the actual crowd collapse zone. You see emergency personnel on their hands and knees administering care, and then evacuating victims, but nothing is explained. All you can gather from the montage is that there was a good time, and then something went very wrong.

The truth is that despite the abundance of footage from the event, none of it clearly catches what happened in the area just outside the Karl-Lehr Street tunnel, where the people went down. There's plenty of video of the underpass filled to capacity, and people using a staircase, a lamppost, and the shipping container to climb out of the throng, but none of it shows the moment when a group of people, near the wall to the left of the staircase, crumples under competing pressures. A depression can be seen in the videos at the time of the collapse—an absence of heads where they were visible in previous shots—and outstretched hands can be glimpsed, reaching out for help, but the crowd surrounding the fallen blocks the view, and no video has emerged that looks straight down from the top of the underpass.

It appears that the crowd became overfocused on reaching the various improvised escape points, even though procedures to disperse the jam were already succeeding in reducing the dangerous densities. In one eyewitness video, you can see people continuing to struggle towards the staircase and the lamppost, while thirty feet behind them the crowd has already cleared, and people are already able to move freely.

It was cool to see the event site in person and get a better impression of the layout. There's a limit to what can be understood from maps and photos on monitors. Boehm and Lutz had been there many times and pointed out exactly where the casualties occurred. Cars zipped over the spot on the street while we looked down on it from the top of the tunnel.

Obsessed with the way cell phones are changing human behavior, Lutz talked some more about what they're calling *sousveillance*, the inverse of *surveillance*. Everybody monitoring what's going on from below, as opposed to being observed from above.

She says that our phone use constitutes a revolution in
evolution that in some ways will equal our jump to conscious
thought. Because the idea of self requires a personal mirror,
the data that the cell phone revolution provides scientists
amounts to a huge societal mirror—humans are beginning the
largest jump in understanding that we've ever experienced.
She says by the time we crunch all the algorithms and figure
out everything there is to figure out about the data we've
already produced, we'll be like another, more advanced version
of our genus.

Lutz had great vocabulary that she used while going on about
the changes coming to medicine, sociology, and psychology.
Borrowing heavily from physics, she used words like *boundary
condition* and *phase transition* to explain the leap in understanding, and she was fond of the term *metaknowledge* to
describe the ability of cell phone users to assess the quality of
the information they were receiving.

She said that if the cell networks hadn't crashed during the
Love Parade, and people had been able to supplement their
info about the circumstances, perhaps Duisberg's crowd crush
incident would have been avoided.

Boehm said Lutz is always trying to "ontologize everything,"
and that she's not sure about including cell phones in the
progression from "ape to God," but that certainly the data is
growing faster than we can study it. She said Facebook alone
creates more statistics on human behavior than all the world's
sociologists can process, and the numbers are only growing.

From my metageek perspective, these guys were really cool, and I was sorry to be wrapping it up with them. We finished our measurements, and they gave me a ride back to my hotel, where I surfed German cable for a few hours, went downstairs and ate in the café, then boned up on my questions for the next day, before passing out with some Ambien.

The university's cafeteria served as the spacious, neutral meeting place for the interviews which began the next morning. I was going with a subset of my online snowball sampling, and a semi-structured interview style. I had a simple map of the festival grounds on which the subjects could trace out their movements, and my list of questions included such things as whether or not waves of force were felt sweeping through the crowd, whether at any point the subjects were unable to use their hands or were lifted off their feet, and whether or not at any moment they had trouble breathing. After my initial queries, I would open it up and ask the subjects to tell me about their experiences unprompted. During the planning stage I considered seeking corroboration of their testimonies, but I gave up on it.

Lately I've wondered what use it is to try and prove anything anymore. Who's to say I'm not making this whole thing up? Where's the line between verity and verisimilitude? You either believe me or you don't.

The first of the interviewees was a Dutch student named Inge who was studying nursing at the university here. She had an isosceles nose, and held her cigarette lighter the whole time, like she couldn't wait to get outside and smoke again.

A one-word summary of her experience at the Love Parade might be "disbelief." Maybe it was her limitations in English that caused her to repeat it, but she kept saying she couldn't believe it. She said she kept thinking, "What are the odds?" as the crowd got progressively tighter around her and her friends, and "this isn't happening" is what she repeated in her mind during the worst of it. She remembers letting out a scream in Dutch, "DIT IS NIET GEBEURT!"

I felt my own pulse quicken while she described it, and I was on the verge of freaking out a little bit.

But she made it out just fine. Nothing *did* happen to her, and she was right about the odds—she escaped them. And when nothing transpires it's easy to see the dangers flip to internalized and invisible things. Creatures of the mind. Are they even there? Just like my own problems. Panic attacks caused by things that don't even exist. Probabilities that washed over and were gone.

More and more studies are demonstrating the existence of mirror neurons, which help to explain the emotional contagion I was experiencing. While performing experiments with macaque monkeys, researchers discovered that certain regions of the brain get lit up when you see *or* perform an action, giving refreshed credence to the old adage, "monkey see, monkey do." The mechanism is not fully understood but it appears that the perception of an action might be the greater part of its execution, that the brain shares neural images for the visualization *and* the realization of various behaviors, so that

imagining something has many of the same effects neuro-
chemically as something actually happening.

As the concept spills over into the realms of language and
thought, we see it propose explanations for empathy and au-
tism, when the mirrors are functioning "normally," and when
they're working overtime. Perhaps sufferers of social anxiety
disorders like myself have mirror neurons that work *too* well.
Because the cognitions and actions of those around us are
shared to a perverse extent, phantom circuits can be firing all
the time, too loud. Swarms of conflicting imitative resonant
behaviors, everything encountered in abstract, overwhelming
the confused experiencer.

Even if you don't think you have problems, you can see it
at work when you're dreaming and the system jumps a rail.
It jerks you awake with the actual action that you visualized
performing in your fantasy. You trip over something in your
dreams and your body kicks awake. The potential is hardwired
into all of us.

Elbert was my next interviewee, a German dude with dread-
locks and a comparatively blobby nose. He was very chatty,
and popped vitamin D supplements while going on about his
current project taking photos of unused playgrounds built
overseas by the US military. He never seemed to stop moving, and kept fiddling with his keys, which he had on a chain
connected to his oversized pants.

He explained that he was under the influence of MDMA
during the Love Parade, and that his experiences were mostly

of euphoria and bewilderment. He was never scared because he couldn't imagine anything really bad happening. He and his friends stayed "up" throughout the event, attempting to spread the message that everything was going to be okay.

I did not overly empathize with him as he described what occurred. I thought about the theories that our particular human consciousness arose from the use of psychoactive plants. "Mind as side effect" has been proposed by various authors, and a derailment of the mirror neuron system looks like a probable suspect. V.S. Ramachandran, the Indian-American neuroscientist, has considered the concept that our self-awareness arises from our mirror neurons looking back at themselves, a mirror-in-a-mirror kind of effect. A malfunction or a hallucinogenic diet might just be the origin of the feedback loop. "We" might be creative solutions to the problem that "we" invented, and each of us, every self, is the product of our own cytoarchitectonic fate, of branching bits of energy that might choose to go one way or another.

Conversely, Kafka said that we're suicidal thoughts that come into God's head.

After creating itself in a hall of mirrors, the mind wants to organize itself, toward a more comprehensible whole. A simplification. Maybe this is where choices come in.

Is it possible that our decisions are byproducts of the mind, itself a byproduct, and that all we're doing is classifying things into dendritic patterns of either/or options? But say it all encodes to zeros and ones, or lefts and rights, and you have to see that the zero stands for nothing, and that the left stands for not-right, that it all boils down to nothings and antipodes. This is the place where information relies on its opposite, the absence of information. Nothingness, not being, is where all the decisions have been made, a negative echo of Hamlet's famous interrogative.

Maybe life is just decisions, but perhaps the decisions forge a tendency toward a continuation of pattern and organization, instead of letting everything burn out to patternlessness. Perhaps decisions exist as the universe's only weapon against entropy.

It's hard not to think that everything's a thermodynamic choice between more and less complicated, that we're on what's most likely the losing team fighting for somethingness, and that one day it will return to ultimate incomprehensibility.

After Elbert, the next interviewee was Ilia, a technology worker from Essen, and she had mink eyes, like tiny twin black holes. She held her flip phone in her hand throughout the exchange, and as she recounted her experiences at the Love Parade she got mad as fuck. The young men around her during the crush were drunk, and drugged, and obnoxious, and she couldn't see much of what was going on except for ass-holes pushing and being dumb. It raised her ire more and more as she talked about it, and I started feeling like she was mad at me. I tried to turn it around and mirror her, like I'm mad too, instead of getting uncomfortable.

There's a famous essay by Jacques Lacan that talks briefly

about an experiment in which pigeons raised in isolation fail
to come to maturity. Without meeting images of themselves,
or other individuals of their species, the birds have no template upon which to finish their development, and they never
realize their biological potential. Placing a mirror or a picture
of a pigeon in their cage is the only thing required for them to
advance, for their gonads to develop, and the implications are
spectacular. In a very real way, what we see is what we are, and
the ramifications extend from medicine to fine art.

At times like this, I try to become the person across from me.
Why can't Ilia's fierceness become my own?

Lacan's essay goes on to be about the formation of our sense
of self during infancy, about how we recognize ourselves in
a mirror, and find a place to paste together our fragmented
experiences into a whole, into an I, something Lacan sees as
a necessary misinterpretation. Because consciousness really
is a mash-up of disparate data—the real, the imaginary, the
symbolic—the ego might be a convenient site to house a resolution to the conflicting inputs.

Unfortunately, we become alienated from ourselves when
we invent a self to play dress-up with, and like the reflection
in the mirror, or like another person whom we might mimic,
the "other" enters the picture in our minds. Being able to
look at your self means there are two selves, and the other
self is made up of just that, otherness. "*Je est un autre*," wrote
Rimbaud. To Lacan this is where the fiction begins, where the
drama that is to be our reality commences, and it's exactly what causes all the mental problems. Too frequently the

illusion breaks down and the mind can't handle the juxtaposi-
tion of self and not-self. Manias and depressions and all other
sorts of phobias and syndromes erupt from the confusion,
from the broken box of mirrors with its shards of phantoms,
and aborted and deformed selves. Lacan believed we're a
paranoid species, born with a "primordial discord," and the
majority of us will fail at performing the roles which society
tries to cast upon us; will fail to live up to the invented images
of ourselves.

Most of Lacan's stuff doesn't really make a lot of sense to me.
He sounds like a prick. His vocabulary is esoteric and estrang-
ing, but I really appreciate his presumption that self-con-
sciousness starts us off in a fictional direction.

I failed in my attempt to imitate Ilia's anger. Her piercing
black eyes burned right through me while she searched for
the words with which to go off in English. She said the big
guys with their little "dickies" kept drinking beer and being
"clod sacks" the whole time she was trapped in the crowd,
and I thought she was going to smash her phone on the table
several times while she related it all.

She was seething, but nothing inside me churned or boiled
when I tried to parrot her rage. I kept looping back to the fact
that she scared me.

My next interviewee matched the descriptions of one of the
rowdy drunk assholes Ilia had been furious with. Alfred was a
twenty-year-old German who admitted that he was drinking
heavily with his friends the day of the Love Parade. He was

a business major, and in the US he might be described as a
frat boy. His arms were so long they seemed awkward, and he
picked lint out of the pockets of his hoodie while we talked.
He said he and his friends couldn't stop laughing the whole
time they were held by the crowd, and that he remembers
chanting local soccer hooligan fight songs with them. With
half of my interviewees so far admitting to being under the
influence of drugs and alcohol during the Love Parade, I began
to question the validity of my sample group, and of any sample group. Who isn't under the influence of something?

But then there was Olga, the subject of my fifth and final
interview, and she was Alfred's opposite. She was small, with
dark curly hair, and she had almost no chin. She held her
hands in a sort of meditative pyramid shape most of the time
we talked, and her arms seemed unusually short. She was not
using drugs or alcohol during the festival, and remained calm
while she was in the crush.

I considered that maybe for every asshole in the crowd
there's someone else radiating love and calm. Picturing mirror
matter, I imagined that all of our particles have their invisible, unknowable opposites. The evidence demonstrates that
the universe is left-handed, that everything tends to spin in
one direction, not the other, and mirror matter might be its
right-handed counterpart. Some theorists like to call it shadow matter, or Alice matter, and there are those who suggest it
is the time-space continuum itself, going in reverse.

Maybe if we could see into mirror matter it would be easier
to see the future because we'd be looking at what already

happened, like watching a movie backward. On the other side, cognition would be cause instead of side effect, and the information that constitutes us would be progressively erased and lost, in a place where the ghost comes before the being. Where all the decisions are undone, there are no decisions to make. Our fragmented mash-up of misinterpretations, our primordial discord, would turn into ultimate understanding and harmony.

It reminds me of the descriptions of prions I've read. The strange infectious agents they've discovered behind mad cow disease, and the human version, Creutzfeldt-Jakob disease, are proteins that curl the wrong way, impeding normal processes, making a mess of the body's chemistry, and encouraging other proteins to wind up the wrong way and become useless too. It might be a good thing that what the monkey sees in the mirror stays on the other side of the looking glass, so it can't reduplicate its misfolded state here, can't pass on its incoordination.

Olga said she tried not to think of any of it while it was happening. She tried to focus on other things. She said she believes we choose our personal histories, that we're in control of our narratives about ourselves and who we are, so it's important not to frame them in a bad light. If all you have is negative details to construct your story, you end up with a negative story.

She remembers people dancing in the distance, and the smiles that broke out despite the frightful situation, and birds flying free overhead. She said she'd read about how there are two selves, the one that experiences, and the one that remembers, and that consciousness goes back and forth between the two. Or maybe three, if you count the unconscious world of dreams as another consciousness. There's probably others too, she said. Making something into a story is equivalent to giving something meaning, and those who are able to can shape their story, and thus its meaning. She said it was weird, but it was all in a book she had read about eldercare—her grandmother has dementia—and empowering the elderly to choose their own path at the end of their lives is an important way to improve end of life care. The conclusion is easier when we see our life as a complete story, when it has meaning. She said if she's going to be the author of her life it's got to be a good read, whether or not it turns out well.

After she was gone and I was finishing my notes, I thought about verb tenses, how our language is structured along the same lines as the different selves: the first person present tense of things happening to yourself versus the third person past tense of telling what happened to someone else. And I thought about all the artifice that comes along with invented narrative structures. Telling yourself a story about your life requires bending, amending, augmenting, rearranging, or deleting certain truths to make it work.

That led to thoughts about how we can only see our reverse in the mirror, while everyone else sees us unflipped, so the mirror image itself is a story. Maybe what's on the other side of the mirror is the opposite of story. Perhaps mirror matter is where everything gets unwritten. Maybe the world without story is where it all goes backward, where it is unwoven and undone. It's where the train is going the other direction, rolling up destiny instead of rolling it out, the opposite of emergence, where all the deaths, and crashes, and tragedies, get disentangled. Where the complexity of everything gets less dense, and isn't a tightening gnarl.

In the mirror, left becomes right and right becomes left, but up stays on the top and down remains on the bottom. This troubles me, and it seems to me to be one of the ultimate paradoxes. How does the image reverse itself in one way but not the other?

Back at my hotel room, I saw myself in the mirror, sitting on the bed typing, and I became unsettled again. Tomorrow I'll stay in Amsterdam overnight before my flight out of Schiphol to Mumbai. The impending increase in population density disturbs my thoughts. I try to feel indifferent toward my reflection, but it seems like it's unwatching me write this, and I imagine on the alternative side of the looking glass the writing gets unwritten as it is written, the story unfolds the other way, toward meaninglessness.

In the otherwhere, as I type it is untyped, as I hit post, it is unposted.

Sending.

AMSTERDAM

October 6, 2011

circumambulation   concentric canals

experimental fiction   fear of drowning

hajj   hajj lit

reverse narrative   short algorithmic descriptions

Stoning the Devil   vestibular system

Click on a point a bit further down the street and fly forward. Pedestrian faces are already blurred purposely by the algorithm, but during the jump, the street and buildings get stretched and distorted too. Stop at the corner of Warmoesstraat and Oudebrugsteeg, in front of The Baba Coffeeshop. Google Street View even allows you to go inside by clicking on the café's façade. A small photo gallery takes you on a quick tour of the bar and the lounge, or perhaps by the time you read this, and check it out in the mapping app, the shop will be boarded up, with a faceless junkie passed out in the doorway.

I've been hiding in a booth in the back here since I arrived from Duisburg this morning. Initially I attempted to avoid the crowds at Central Station by exiting to the north, against the flow, but I was blocked by the oddly spelled IJ River nearing the end of its journey outside the north exit, and the options appeared bleak to the east and west. Some women who looked like they might be prostitutes were smoking cigarettes on the north steps, and I retreated back through the station, joined the rabble for a few blocks south, then found the first place that looked good for coffee and Wi-Fi, The Baba.

Viewing it now, from above with the map program, I see all the concentric, semicircular canals of the city feed into the IJ on its southern bank, and it reminds me of the human vestibular system, with its labyrinth of loops. The connections they've discovered between agoraphobia and the inner ear remain unexplained, but it makes sense to me that the seat of our balance and orientation might be the source of my problems with panicking in public. It's like a dizziness of thought that overcomes me when I slip into an episode, and the nebulous notions accompanying the breakdowns loop around and around.

Some guys were smoking a spliff at the next table, and for a few minutes I thought I was slipping into a contact high, resonant contagious brainwave frequencies pulling me into the whorl again. I calmed down by doing some random math problems in my head while staring at the hibiscus flowers nearby on the bar. It's been a while since I did the Panic and Agoraphobia Scale questions recommended by my therapist, so I pulled them up on-screen and went through them. I got a score very close to my normal, and it was reassuring that my travels weren't throwing me into a higher bracket, but the numbers didn't match up with what I was feeling. Tomorrow I will arrive in Mumbai, and I have serious concerns about my ability to maintain my cool so far outside my element.

When I was at the bar getting more coffee, I was sucked into a short conversation with a Hollander who pegged me for an American. After I explained that I'm a sociologist researching human stampedes, he told me about his work as a plumber and a roofer. He said in the Netherlands they're the same thing because they're both about water management, and he showed me a patch on his jacket indicating his certification. Apparently one of the world's foremost hydrology programs is in the Netherlands, which makes sense for a country where large regions are below sea level. Indeed, you can't go very far without crossing a canal in these parts. He said there's almost as many *grachten* in Dutch colloquialisms as there are *fietsen*.

"It's easy to forget we're underwater here, but if you pay attention you can feel it," he said. "There's always going to be a bigger flood, one that overwhelms the levees and the dams. What's important is that you're prepared to pump out again!"

Getting back to my booth, I thought about how when the flood comes, I'll stay holed up in my sanctum and I'll drown.

Before I left the States, my so-called girlfriend said that traveling to foreign lands is like taking LSD. It makes the mind more open to experiences. But what about when all you want to do is hide from the next experience?

She also said Buddhists say it takes the soul ten to twelve days to catch up to your body when you travel, which would put mine right in the middle of the shitstorm phone call with her back in Arenas de Cabrales. If you keep moving does it ever catch up?

I see myself reflected in the laptop screen, and I am still the same loser that I was last week. I could be out exploring how cool Amsterdam is, but I'm squirreled away a few blocks from the train. I could be looking at Van Goghs, or touring the Rijksmuseum, or taking a peek at the over-hyped Red Light District, or peering down into the glass-floored houseboats along the waterways, or doing heroin with hipsters, but...

When I checked my emails, I found that a friend who's been reading my blog sent me a link to another blog about agoraphobia, called "A Traveling Agoraphobic." I absorbed the whole pitiful chronicle, and then sank to the bottom.

In seventeen short posts that cover the course of three months last year, the blog goes from demoralized to below hopeless, as its anonymous narrator recounts her terrifying minor outings, attempting to come to terms with the panic attacks she has in public. At the end of it, she becomes sick, and then it turns out she's sick because she's pregnant, and in the final post she expresses complete desperation and misery about what she can do before falling silent.

Of course the blog formatting stacks her posts in reverse, so the narrative runs backward. This is exactly what I was talking about in my first blog entry. Her story starts off with the most recent post and—BAM!—done. The end. Complete and horrible silence. Why bother digging any further down the stack into salmon recipes and lists of her personal coping mechanisms? It's like spying on the last pages of a mystery first. The right-now fills in all the gaps from the before, and renders the rest redundant. She isn't improving, she loses her shit, and it's over.

By the time I finished reading the whole of it, I realized what a great piece of experimental fiction it might make. An exercise in everything one wants on page one, and no reason to read the rest. Everything else is just particulars. Did the author simply make the whole thing up without leaving the room? Is it contaminated with fiction? Riddled with the imaginary? Are those places you're allowed to go?

It's not lost on me that tomorrow I will be flying over the Arabian Peninsula, where the hajj will be in full swing in about a month. The hajj is the largest annual pilgrimage on earth, and Mecca is the world's unofficial crowd crush capital, but I'm prohibited from doing crowd research there because infidels are not allowed to visit Mecca and its sacred sites. I can only experience the hajj in a mediated way, like reading a travel blog. Although no discussion about crowd crush would be complete without some words on the hajj, I'm forced to rely on the testimony of others in order to give my reader an overview.

So, if we're to believe the accounts, the hajj is the biggest yearly gathering on the planet, with an estimated three million people participating in Mecca this year. Since Saddam Hussein is gone from power in Iraq, there are rumblings that the Arbaeen pilgrimage to Karbala might soon surpass the hajj's numbers, but for now the hajj is the biggest. There are larger gatherings in India, like the Kumbh Mela, with one hundred million participants over a two-month period, and perhaps thirty million visiting Haridwar in one day, but none of the massive Indian get-togethers are yearly events. Around a third of the hajj's pilgrims already reside in Saudi Arabia, with the remaining two million crossing international borders to participate. Sporting events, festivals like Burning Man, or political protests like Occupy are the only places most Americans will witness anything remotely similar without leaving their own country, but the numbers don't really come close. Perhaps the worsening US plutocracy will eventually cause protest events in North America where the attendance adds up in the millions, but for now apathy and atheism reign.

Before reading more about it, I was like most Americans, and only knew that Muslims go to Mecca, and walk in circles around a little black building, and pray. I didn't realize that it takes about seven days, requires the performance of a complex multitude of rituals, and that guides and guidebooks are indispensable for a successful experience. Indeed, a fair percentage of hajj-goers are hired attendants, lucky that their jobs help assure their own arrivals in heaven.

The Mecca region was the prophet Mohammad's old stomping ground, and when one performs the hajj, one is repeating a series of actions that he performed in the year 632 CE, not long before he died. Hundreds of years before Mohammad grew up here, Abraham's faith was tested in the same desertic terrain, when God asked Abraham to sacrifice his son, and

then let him get away with slaughtering a ram and circumcis-
ing all the dudes in his clan instead. A little while after that,
he abandoned his wife Hagar and their son Ishmael nearby,
in what was at that time the middle of nowhere. It helps to
know about Abraham, and Ishmael, and Hagar if you're talking
about the hajj, because many of the rituals involve acting out
parts of their stories.

Apparently, the whole Islam thing got started when
Mohammad was hanging out by himself in a cave a few miles
outside of Mecca and he started to hallucinate. An angel
clutched him and ordered him to recite, and much of what
he declaimed over the next few years would be collected and
called the Koran. It is interesting to consider the similarities
between Mohammad and Ignatius of Loyola, the founder
of the Jesuits, who I discussed in my post from Montserrat.
Both of them were sometime warriors who eventually laid
down their arms, both of them started religious movements,
and both of them tripped out and had spiritual visions while
hiding by themselves in caves. So what is it about caves that
produce visions and visionaries? I'm reminded of the scene in
A Passage to India, when Adela has hallucinations while visiting
the caverns at Marabar. She imagines she is sexually assaulted
by Dr. Aziz, but really it's the disturbing effects of echoes, and
darkness, and aloneness that assail her. The acoustic effects of
the holy Indian caves are accented in the movie, demonstrating the one existing in the many, as the echoes are returned
manifold and awesome, and they make me think of the little
caverns inside the human ear again. Could there be a connection between malfunctions in the tiny echoing caves inside
our heads, and the propensity toward the visionary? While

Mohammad's cave is not included in the prescribed tour of the sacred sites that make up the hajj proper, it is often visited as a bonus by those who can.

Those who can are obliged to go on the hajj—at least that's how the requirement to perform the hajj is explained to us in the West—but it's much more complicated. Being able to go means being free of all debts and obligations at home—you can't just leave everything behind on a whim and ignore the shit that's piling up while you're being dutifully ascetic. Conversely, simply the intent to go on the hajj may be considered meritorious, if for example you can't leave your ailing mother, but otherwise you could go. One famous imam has even commented that by helping a mother in need, a Muslim gains more heavenly rewards than by going to Mecca. Apparently, making the preparations to go can also count as having gone, should something prevent the trip, and dying in a plane crash while landing at the airport in Jeddah would be considered sufficient. It is assumed that the rituals would have been performed, and those who perish on the way gain the same accolades as those who accomplish the pilgrimage. It seems like an incredibly gracious facet of Islam, that God goes ahead and blesses you for what you *might* have done.

There were times when many people died on the way. Before engine-powered travel, getting to Mecca could be an arduous journey that took weeks, months, and in some cases years. For those coming from afar, the greater part of the hajj was just getting there and back, thus the earliest hajj travel literature consists of mnemonic poems that recall the names and locations of the watering stations and stopping places along the way. The importance of water to overland traffic in this part of the world cannot be overstated, and the extensive resources required to plan and mount a trip across the difficult deserts resulted in an eventual golden age of caravans, when the excursions became traveling cities with tens of thousands of people, in possession of their own markets, security forces, and mini governments.

There are legends of carpets unfurled through the desert ahead of royal pilgrims who never had to touch the ground, and of ice being imported to wealthy sultans in Mecca via the highly efficient transportation networks that evolved. But the arrival of steam power quickly put an end to all that, as ports not far from the Holy City made ocean travel the main mode for foreigners to reach the Arabian Peninsula. Gone are the days of the grand camel columns, and the books of routes and realms that once characterized hajj literature have become anachronisms. How to get to the next oasis and where to camp for the night fell from importance, and hajj lit trans- formed with the changes in transportation into more person- alized accounts of travel by trains, ships, and planes.

In the West, perhaps the most famous written account of the hajj experience comes from Sir Richard Francis Burton, an English geographer who went so far as to get circumcised in order to sneak himself into Mecca in 1853. Because he wasn't a practicing Muslim, Burton's hajj lit is more like *fake* hajj lit, but its importance to the genre is undeniable.

Considering the significance of Abraham's pact with God, and its requisite genital mutilation rites, I think it's of interest that

I've found no mention of circumcision—besides Burton's—in any of my readings about the hajj and its practices. Men come to Mecca from all over the globe, and there's one physical thing that they all share—or should I say *don't* share? So you might imagine that the hajj is like a giant anti foreskin conference, but as far as I can tell, the issue is completely ignored, or at least covered up. Because male circumcision is not common in India, it might be hard to find a circumcised population density anywhere on earth that could compete with Mecca during the pilgrimage. The sky-bound buds of the minarets on the mosques look like the only foreskins in Mecca. Somehow they slip past the censorship. Aliens observing our species might marvel at the miracle that is the great concentration of the circumcised that occurs there annually, without any acknowledgment of the trauma that all the male participants, and a percentage of the women, have in common. Isn't it sort of like all of the world's amputee victims getting together, but none of them saying anything about their missing limbs?

Or maybe they do bring up circumcision in rituals and prayers, but the information is excised by Western writers. Perhaps I should get help translating one of the many virtual hajjs available online, and see if at some point there are offerings, or incantations, or observances for the removal of the penis's protective sheath.

From what I can tell so far, the virtual hajj tours on the internet offer condensed first person point of view episodes that seem to be in interesting opposition to the "all one" concepts celebrated in the pilgrimage. Some of the videos appear to break the whole thing up into chapters, like a passion play, each one focusing on a day and its rites. Watching them, the viewer mirrors the protagonist's actions and participates in a sort of experience transfer. Even though there might be thousands of people on the video screen, the perspective remains essentially eye-level and personal. At least that's what I've seen in the thumbnails. It's doubtful that the handheld camera can express anything but the opposite of the sense of unity achieved when millions act together.

Of course, GPS, the spread of digital Baedeckers, and the rise of the video hajj might put many of Mecca's guide jobs at risk, but considering the continuing problems with ever-increasing attendance, the escalation of the digital pilgrimage might be a good thing. Perhaps the situation will eventually get to the point where the imams sanction virtual hajj as a way to reduce the crowds in Mecca. Right now, things are capped at one thousand visas per million Muslims per country per year, and they're still having problems with too many people. With virtual hajj, travel would become superfluous. Instead of going to the hajj, the hajj could come to you. This would be an interesting reversal since many conservative imams currently see Sheik Google as an unstoppable, liberalizing challenge to traditional localized authorities. But the interwebs might actually make possible an *increase* in religious participation when it comes to the hajj. Perhaps the virtual hajj will eventually be considered more evolved than the real hajj.

After their arrival in Mecca, the pilgrim is considered to be on the hajj starting when they wash and put on the clothes they will wear for the next few days. For the men, it is an unsewn white cloth, the same type of fabric in which the bodies of the dead are wrapped. Participants understand that it is to be a kind of dress rehearsal for death and final judgment that they will perform. They pray, "Lead me with a just ingoing, and lead me out with a just outgoing."

For many it will be their first and only time in the Middle East, and since there are proscriptions against representational depiction in Muslim religious art and architecture, I wonder if some pilgrims arriving for the first time might marvel at the simplified visual environment. I imagine it could be a subtle difference, but perhaps it would be an improvement in the chaos that usually surrounds us. Jürgen Schmidhuber, a German computer scientist, has theorized that beautiful things have short algorithmic descriptions, so we might expect that an overall reduction in visual complexity could enhance what remains. I'm reminded of the "less is more" concept. As someone who suffers from overstimulation in public, I think maybe such cultural prohibitions on ornamentation would help people like me keep my cool. I read somewhere that God's architecture is emptiness, that what cathedrals create is a hollowness where people are more likely to experience holiness, that in some ways what is being replicated is the almighty vacuum of the desert. I imagine the simpler the better, until there's nothing left but overwhelming nothingness, where the whole thing loops back around to despair.

Because the hajj is still tied to lunar cycles, its dates are not fixed and it moves around on the Gregorian calendar. Imams use astronomical data to decide ahead of time on which day the Arafat vigil will occur, and this determines the rest of the schedule. On the first day, the pilgrims travel by foot to the barren Plain of Arafat, or to its hillock, to stand from noon until sundown in contemplation, meditation, and prayer, just like Mohammad once did. The Abraham-sacrificing-Ishmael thing is at the heart of their observances, and the ceremony is considered to be central to the pilgrimage. He who misses the standing at Arafat has missed the hajj.

No matter the weather, the penitents stand throughout the afternoon, symbolically awaiting God's commands. The word *Muslim* means "one who submits," and those gathered at Arafat display their willingness to obey. Apparently, a willingness to await signs and signals from the creator pervades Islam, and a sense of predestination infiltrates the religion's philosophies as well. I'm not the first to consider that it might be liberating, believing your choices don't matter because they've already been made for you, but for the most part I'm not convinced.

It seems strange to me that everyone congregates at Arafat to replicate what was probably a solitary experience for Mohammad. Isn't it possible that he just wanted to be alone in the desert? With so many people there, the desert's vacuum is annihilated, the breathtaking emptiness that made Mohammad's sojourn special is gone. Wouldn't it be better if everyone wandered off into the desert alone? Or perhaps everyone being alone together is the point.

On the way back to Mecca, at a place called Muzdalifa, each pilgrim collects forty-nine pebbles to use in the Stoning of the Devil rituals at the Jamaraats later during the week. The Jamaraats are three freestanding walls that mark three appearances of Shaitan, Islam's Satan, and the stoning ritual requires that the devotees arrive close enough to the walls to hit them with all their pebbles. Because of the close quarters required during the ritual, and because it has to happen multiple times on multiple days, the Stoning of the Devil has been the focal point of numerous fatal incidents, and the area around the Jamaraats must contend for the number one crowd crush site in recorded history.

The Stoning of the Devil takes place at a site outside of Mecca proper, where Shaitan appeared and tried to talk Ishmael out of going along with his father's sacrifice. Ishmael threw rocks at the devil and it vanished. In some accounts it happened to Ishmael twice more, and in other accounts Shaitan tried again with Abraham, and then Hagar, but he was repelled with stones each time.

The Jamaraats were originally simple cairns marking the spots of the encounters with Shaitan, but they were eventually expanded into walls, so that larger crowds could perform the ritual. Because people continued to get injured and die in the crushes trying to reach the walls, the Saudis expanded them upward still further, and built a massive, parking-garage-like structure around them called the Jamaraat Bridge. Not really a bridge per se, because it doesn't cross or connect anything, it's a sort of bridge over itself. Built by Saudi Arabia's premier construction conglomerate, the Bin Laden Group, it is a modern marvel of crowd control experimentation, and now stands five stories tall. Massive on-ramps and off-ramps funnel pilgrims in and out on multiple levels simultaneously, in great sloping curves resembling interstate cloverleafs.

Looking at it from above on Google Earth, it's hard to imagine
that the massive construction is for pedestrian worshippers
to use during only one week of the year—it looks more like
a futuristic freeway transit hub, laid out in a vaguely human
shape. Huge, multilingual, overhead signs resembling those on
superhighways, help the masses merge and disperse. Security
towers abound to monitor flows, and to communicate real or
potential problems—the latest in crowd safety technology has
been engineered into all of it—and they're *still* having problems with crushes during the Stoning of the Devil.

While the Jamaraat Bridge is not really a bridge, it shares the
same problems when it comes to moving dangerously dense
groups of humans. On YouTube, there's fairly good footage
from a few years ago of shockwaves pulsing through tight
crowds in one of the ingress canals. When I watched the
footage, I imagined that if I were stuck upright in the throng,
sardine-packed in the Arabian heat, I might get to thinking
that seeking out the devil to throw rocks at him might not be
such a good idea. In fact, it seems like a pretty good way to
get fucked. There's a Taoist saying about order arising sponta-
neously when things are left alone. Perhaps everyone should
leave the devil be. It makes me wonder if they're exercising or
exorcising their demons.

Of course, the three Jamaraats have become metaphorical
devils, so I shouldn't oversimplify. I've read that the three
targets represent the inner Shaitan of personal choices and
conflicts, the outer Shaitan of real-world devils, and the third
Shaitan is more like the larger, more organized notions of enemies, like religions or nations. Similarly, I have read that the

three Jamaraats represent specifically capitalism, despotism, and religious hypocrisy, so it looks like what you imagine the devils to be depends on which religious school you're coming from.

If you can choose your own stand-ins to expel, I would probably choose the crushing crowd itself as one of the devils, making the whole thing a recursive loop, where the crowd throws rocks at itself until it disappears. To someone with agoraphobia like myself, the crowd might be the biggest devil.

Abraham ended up sacrificing an animal as a substitute for his son Ishmael, and when they're done with the Jamaraats, many pilgrims re-enact his sacrifice. In what must be the world's largest annual bloodletting, thousands of halal butchers slaughter hundreds of thousands of sheep, goats, cows, and camels, with about a third of the meat getting directed to charity. The Saudis have struggled to put in place an efficient infrastructure to process such large amounts of meat and offal in one evening, and imams have greenlighted systems of online animal sacrifice as a way to reduce the logistical carnage. This augurs future concessions toward online religious practices.

Of the various rituals of the hajj, Westerners are most familiar with images of pilgrims circling the square, black building called the Kaaba, and many of the pilgrims will do this *tawāf* three times before the hajj is over, once at the beginning, once after the sacrifices, and again as a farewell. Before Mohammad's ascendancy, there were many competing shrines in Mecca—a spiritual smorgasbord—and he was to have all of the shrines except the Kaaba destroyed, in one of history's most influential acts of literal iconoclasm. Tradition has it that the Kaaba structure was originally built by Adam and was rebuilt by Abraham after the big flood that's in the Bible, and that angels have always circled overhead there ever since God created the earth. Apparently, the site sits directly below God's throne and his celestial home.

There is some disagreement on the origin of the sacred stone that sits mortared into the corner of the Kaaba, and some believe that it fell from heaven, a meteorite. Supposedly it's the same rock that Mohammad was fond of circling and touching back in the seventh century. Seven counterclockwise laps are necessary to complete this ritual, and scholars are fairly certain the rite is a vestige of pre-Islamic practices in the region. Indeed, circumambulation of sacred sites and objects has been found in all the world's religions, although Islam seems to be one of the only ones that goes counterclockwise.

Fascinating research by Rob Cowen demonstrates that without a specific destination, people on an enclosed plane will end up walking in circles. A mesmerizing animation is available online that demonstrates all the red dots, representing people, conforming to mass rotation in a great example of monkey see monkey do. I'm reminded of the famous ant colony optimization algorithms that demonstrate how insects find the shortest distance between food supplies and home. Everyone just keeps walking around, and then a pattern crystalizes.

Circumambulations of the Kaaba are often followed by what's called the *sa'y*, and this is the ritual I can identify with more

than the others. This is the one in which the experiences of
the abandoned Hagar are reenacted. After Abraham left
Hagar and Ishmael alone in the desert without provisions,
ostensibly to die, Hagar panicked and ran back and forth
between two hills, Safa and Marwa, not knowing what to do.
During the *sa'y*, her panic attack is loosely replicated by the
devotees, who take turns running and walking seven times
between the places where Hagar is said to have freaked out.
The entire route, hills and all, is literally inside Mecca's Grand
Mosque now. In ways its interior resembles a huge fancy
mall—air conditioned, serviced by several fast and slow lanes,
and on multiple floors with balconies. The organization of the
crowds at the *sa'y* must be impressive, perhaps more so than
at the Stoning of the Devil, because everyone must hurry, and
the crowd is split going different directions.

Hagar left her baby sitting on the ground and lost her shit,
running around crazed and desperate, and it's quite remarkable that millions repeat her manic breakdown every year,
recognizing her anxiety, her terror, and her trauma. Just
imagine how she felt, abandoned by her husband in the desert
to die. Abraham was a total dick. Actually he was a total dick
minus a foreskin. Crucify me.

When I had my first panic attack, I was afraid I would never
again be free of the things I had seen all at once: a bird that is
somehow all birds, a four-faced angel, a tree at the end of everything, and a thousand places from every angle simultaneously. But language is successive, so it can only be written in
time. Feeling it is the only way to understand it. How radical

of Mohammad to acknowledge Hagar's panic by replicating it
with his own perambulations. How progressive of the prophet
to recognize her perturbation by reenacting it.

Meanwhile, miraculously, while Hagar was nearby freaking
out, little baby Ishmael kicked at the ground and uncovered
the spring that was to become the holiest water source in
Islam, the Zamzam Well. Hagar and her son were saved by the
Zamzam waters in the legend, and Mecca would eventually
grow up from the little spring into what it is today.

It's easy to be suspicious that the legend was superimposed
onto an already existing oasis, but no matter the origin story,
the rare water source in the desperately thirsty region became
the centerpiece of regional power struggles for centuries.
Essentially, whoever controlled the Zamzam water controlled
the hajj.

On the last two days of the pilgrimage, the Stoning of the
Devil and the circumambulation of the Kaaba are repeated,
and then the hajj is completed. When it's over, the participant
is called a *hajji*, so US soldiers deploy the term incorrectly
when they use it to describe random enemy combatants,
especially since it is a designation of respect.

More than 1,400 people died during a crush incident in
Mecca in 1990, and despite improvements in facilities,
experts predict more problems. Already the numbers are un-
manageable. Population increase points to a time not far from
now when so many devotees will be turned away from the hajj
that one of the five pillars of the religion will prove generally

unattainable as it is currently practiced. It is obvious that Islam has a growth problem.

The Population Division of the UN says we're going to reach seven billion people on the planet this October, and the number's rise will bring a corresponding increase in the number of deaths worldwide. The current fifty-seven million deaths per year is scheduled to climb to over eighty million by 2040, and it's like I can feel the flood of death inching up incrementally while I keep hiding in this booth at the back of the café. We are surrounded by water, and the unremitting deluge gains ground. Tomorrow I will be in India, and I foresee myself in a sea of bodies, drowned. Mumbai's density is estimated at twenty-one thousand souls per square kilometer.

Sending.

MUMBAI

October 8, 2011

2011 Tōhoku Earthquake and Tsunami   Abelian sandpile

Angel of Oblivion   Kali Yuga

mandala   Mount Meru

nutation   Sorites paradox

supervenience   Towers of Silence

The bright yellow tram to Schipol at sunrise, the Air India flight, customs at Chhatrapati, the trippy taxi ride, the hotel, and now another café so I can use the internet. Each constituent is stacked on the last one, and while you might remove any one part from the whole without it collapsing, like a game of Jenga, there must be some minimum of matrix or you don't have a narrative.

The Air India logo involves the rudder of an airplane morphed with the shape of a bird. More or less a red, caudated triangle, with half of a golden starburst inside it on the leading edge. The tails of the 787s at the gates mirrored the airline's logo, creating a mild Droste effect upon entering the plane, as if I were inside the logo.

The seats were a rich red, with a dull gold pattern of pais-
ley-like shapes, in accord with the airline's crimson branding,
and very similar to Spain's federal color scheme. A little tur-
baned mascot appeared on the inflight magazines, the safety
instructions, and the snacks. He repeated the color palette in
his robe, his headwear, and his genie shoes. A huge handlebar
mustache completed his mildly racist appearance. With the
flight crew's attire replicating the reds again, it felt like a bit of
an overdose of vermilion. Is this what you're supposed to write
about when you're traveling?

Soon the ground began to flash away between breaks in clouds,
then it was gone completely as we rose through white, and in a
brilliant burst a few minutes later we came out on top of them,
a rippled sea of wispy milky waves below blueness, everything
simplified. While the airport's crowds were mildly disturbing,
the airplane's paddocked passengers didn't bother me as much
this time, and as it was to be a long flight, I planned to tranquil-
ize myself heavily and sleep through it. This must be travel writing at its best, when the author is counting sheep through the
action. Nobody really wants to read about the flight anyway.

Wait, scroll back up again for a second. I can talk about the
before, when the future was on its way and already tied to
what was the present, even while staying stationary. It is coming at you, even while you are motionless. Sitting in the airport going zero miles an hour is still terrifying, perhaps more
terrifying, because dying at five-hundred miles an hour makes
sense, but sitting there motionless before the flight causes the
dying later, and doesn't make any sense at all. It's when you're
sitting there before the flight that you might exercise your

exit option. Once you're in the air, the future won't care what decisions you made or make.

From the hostel in Amsterdam to the hostel in Mumbai, I traveled around four thousand miles today, and even while sitting still in the airport I averaged more than one hundred miles an hour. In situations like these, slowing down might prevent certain contingencies but cause others. Like when the airplane falls out of the sky because it's not going fast enough.

Was that sandalwood or spices I smelled in the dry air after we landed and they opened up the airplane? Am I an asshole if I describe the odors as exotic? Is one allowed to consider anything exotic anymore, or am I an Orientalist for simply noticing the differences? How does one write about being in a new place without nodding toward dissimilitude? Why shouldn't I say something about the very air, when my fellow passengers all seemed to breathe deeper and take comfort in it as it blew through the cabin?

There was an incredibly long walk to customs, with a smattering of the nation's arts and crafts on the walls along the way, and there were around forty serviceable counters where they could process passports, but only two of them open despite lengthy lines.

Just as I feared beforehand, outside of customs is when things started to get difficult. I'm farthest from shore here in India, right about halfway around the globe from Seattle, being everything I can be, or faking it more than ever. I will muddle through.

I had done my research, I knew to get a taxi to my hotel in the Historic District as there are no tuk-tuks allowed in the old part of downtown. It was a very clean example of the famous Premier Padmini, a black body with yellow top and tags. The hood emblem consisted of a chrome chevron capped with a red tent-shaped trapezoid in which the silvery letters "PAL" leaned to the right, suggesting movement I assume. There was lots of horn honking, but that doesn't seem like something that needs to be explained. A woman stepped out in front of the cab at one point, forcing the driver to slam the brakes. Glancing at me in the rearview, he shook his head disappointedly and said, "Fucking Kali Yuga man, fucking Kali Yuga."

I wondered about the symbolism in the different tilaks that I saw on foreheads, and then I wondered, should I bother writing about the cows, bikes, and rickshaws? The beggars and vendors? Aren't those things already a given when talking about India? Do I mention the rice, and the masala dosas? Or is the average reader already familiarized with the basics of Indian cuisine, so my recounted experiences only confirm my colonialist perspective?

Do I mention fig trees?

The local buses bear an insignia that says "BEST," and I asked the driver about it. He said it stands for Bombay Electric Service and Transport. Its two red arrows arc clockwise around a white light bulb, inside of which floats the image of a red bus. I found that thinking about the Devnagri script underneath the emblem as purposefully undecipherable graffiti helped with my feelings of incomprehension. For that matter,

all the non-English signage everywhere could be looked at as
coded graffiti that I'm not supposed to get because I'm not in
the club.

I had already been warned about the imperfections of India.
My friend in the department had seen things on her recent
travels that had disturbed her. She saw a woman with her feet
on backward, and what she could only describe as a half a
man. She told me about seeing an American wearing a "Life
Is Good" T-shirt while walking through one of the poorer
neighborhoods of Calcutta, and she told me to try not to
be that dickhead. I started to judge my own actions in India
long before I actually arrived in country, and now the level of
self-analysis felt terrifying. So I just sat there and looked out.
What else do you do in a taxi?

I thought about Sartre saying that the essence of reality is
scarcity, that there's not enough of anything to go around,
and I considered that what I lacked was a place to be alone. I
wanted to get to my hostel and be alone. Didn't someone else
say reality is the original Rorschach test? What other things
can you compare reality to?

My quaint and modern hostel was just a few blocks from the
grand and historic Taj Hotel, which played a leading role in the
horror that Indians call 26/11, the terrorist attacks in Mumbai
that began on the twenty-sixth of November three years ago.
Consisting of twelve coordinated assaults on sites throughout
the Mumbai metro area, the events left at least one-hundred
seventy-four dead and more than three-hundred wounded.
Many Americans probably haven't heard of 26/11, and might

not understand why it's not called 11/26, but it was more or less India's 9/11. I'll add terrorist attacks, and pogroms in their aftermath, to my growing list of things to try to not worry about.

From my room's small balcony I saw a vulture cruise over the neighborhood, and I was reminded of a recent article in Harper's Magazine about the Towers of Silence not far away to the northeast. For centuries, the area's Zoroastrian community has placed their deceased in the open air atop these structures to be consumed by vultures, but lately the system is breaking down. There are too many bodies, or not enough vultures, and various theories abound as to which element of the arrangement has led to the failure. It reminds me of the problems with the hajj to Mecca, and with other pilgrimages. Too many people for the ritual to work, and then bodies piling up. One of the leading theories about the vultures postulates high levels of opioids in the Zoroastrian corpses causing health problems for the birds. This makes me think about soaring over Mumbai while on OxyContin, and about how this whole fucking thing is about flying while sedated.

Zoroaster was a predecessor of Ignatius of Loyola in the way he thought all our tiny choices are decisions between good and evil, between gods of lightness and darkness. He had visions of angels and demons too, and believed that in the struggle between Asha and Druj—between order and deception—one should seek and assist Asha. That's Zoroaster's big takeaway. He is considered by some to be the world's first philosopher, and his "worship of wisdom" became the word "philosophy" in Greek. It has been suggested that his teachings about an individual's moral choices, heaven and hell, resurrection of the body, last judgment, and everlasting life, have all been recycled into today's Abrahamic religions, that Muslims, Jews, and Christians have all dipped into Zoroaster's well of wisdom. He was a mega-free-will kind of guy. To him we are not slaves to fate but choose our paths, and we either make the world a better place or worse. But I don't find this point of view freeing, I find it crippling. Was I free? Am I free?

And doesn't the everything-is-good-or-evil of Zoroaster, and others, just equate to the everything-is-zeros-or-ones of meaningless and forgotten files? Of course there are those, like the followers of the *Principia Discordia*, who believe all dichotomies to be false dichotomies, illusions created by perspectives, but that doesn't explain how a computer reads binary code, and then how those bits and bytes get forgotten.

The vulture tipped out of sight over rooftops, and I wondered if thinking about the larger topic of death is classified as worrying. If you're thinking about someone else's death, or everyone's deaths, or how a society deals with it, are you necessarily thinking about your own? I've got to run my PAS numbers later and I want to be honest with myself about how much I'm freaking out.

Buddhism has got its Nine Cemetery Contemplations, the Satipatthana Sutta. The text contains the instructions for monks in observing the nine phases of a body's decomposition over many months of visits to a charnel ground. Apparently the exercises aren't over until the mindful witness is forced to smile while contemplating the bones turned back to dust. To nothing.

While reading about agoraphobia back home I stumbled on references to the Aghori of India, a grouping of sadhus which has been described as a death sect, consisting of ascetics who occupy the charnel grounds along the Ganges. It is said that they eat the unburned parts of the dead after funeral pyres, allowing the spirit to be completely purified, and they have been reported sitting and meditating atop corpses, painting themselves with the ashes of burned bodies, and drinking from human skulls. But when I mentioned some of these details to Harish, my officemate back in Seattle, whose parents are from Bangalore, he looked disappointed and said, "Don't believe everything you read on the internet."

Whether there's any truth-value in those particular stories doesn't matter much, it is for sure that there are some tripper old sadhus hanging out in Varanasi. From what little I know, Hinduism doesn't put much stock in "truth" anyway, and it's got other things going for it as well. It's got all the little gods that make up the big ones. They've still got a pantheon, with all the millions of supporting roles, allowing for all the overlap. The gods add up over cyclical ages exponentially and become a pile of gods, and each individual god is just a miniature of the heap.

But there's this thing about supervenience, about stacking. There's always an up. Everything seems to pile up on everything else, not down on everything else. My death in a plane crash on the way here wouldn't happen without first surviving the tram to the airport, but surviving the tram doesn't depend on surviving the plane. Or does it?

Right now I'm having coffee and using the internet at a
franchise of Café Coffee Day. Apparently the chain is popular
throughout India. The art on the walls depicts hip-looking
young Indians holding oversized, pro-coffee text message cut-
outs. One says, "A lot can happen over coffee," yet nothing
is happening. I am not seeing India, I am hiding in a familiar
environment. It looks like a Starbucks, but with a Seattle's
Best color scheme. The walls are red brick, but they look too
perfect to be real.

Thinking about the way things create piles reminds me of
Charles Perrow's book *Normal Accidents*. Like the pioneering
research on crowds that Dirk Helbing did, discussed in my
post from Duisburg, Perrow's book is considered a seminal
text on complex systems failures. He demonstrates that in
certain types of organizations, large accidents are rare, but
inevitable and normal, and that efforts to increase the safety
of a system might actually decrease it, because of a greater
overall complexity. In many cases complexity ensures failure, and more complex means more categories of accidents
too. Things are put into risky relationships with each other,
where there's both tight and loose coupling. Think Bhopal,
Chernobyl, Challenger, and what Perrow calls the quintessen-
tial systems accident, Y2K. Complexity can be organized, and
it just might reach a state of self-organized criticality, with its
resultant, unanticipated, cascades of failure. I realize that *I'm*
a normal accident, that thinking about everything that can
happen might ensure my failure.

Perrow's book introduced me to the Abelian sandpile, or the
Bak-Tang-Wiesenfeld model if you prefer. It's a computer

program that drops imaginary grains of sand over a grid, and graphs the data as various types of heaps form on the matrix. With the right parameters dialed in, the pile of sand will reach a steady state of continual collapse, little avalanches occurring in concentric patterns on its surface, and the shape of the dunes will remain fixed, even with an exponential increase in size. Despite the random nature of where the individual grains fall, the same pretty mosaic emerges. The grains topple onto their neighbors, and arrive at a stable configuration of instability. In each sector, adding one more grain might do nothing, or it might cause its zone to collapse onto others—a massive slide made of many little ones.

This can lead to thoughts about what exactly stability is. There's much ado about it, but demonstrating its existence is problematic. Think of the most stable thing you know, and then imagine turning off the gravity. Turn off attraction, turn off repulsion, and what kind of soup does it all become? They say the sandpile is "attracted to its critical state," but aren't we all?

In any case, if you're talking about how to avoid accidents, it's not the individual grain of sand that you should fear, but the *system* being in a state that's ready to slide, like my brain feeling ready to be submerged at any moment.

In an earlier time, moments were counted with sand. Five minutes was forty ounces of it in a standard hourglass. I think the Abelian model might be another way to look at time. The model also displays pink noise, a vibration pattern common to many complex systems in nature. With the right color coding for the probabilities, some images of the sandpiles display perfect mandalas.

But what about running it in reverse? Then you get the sorites paradox. The paradox of the heap. A fourth century BCE thinker from Anatolia, Eubulides of Miletus, is said to have wondered at what point a heap is still a heap if you remove it grain by grain. If all that's left is a few kernels scattered around does it constitute anything? Is it still a heap when only one remains?

The word *sorites* is simply the Greek for heap, and thinking about the conundrum has led to discussions about the truth-value gap, and fuzzy hedges, and vague predicates. There's a tension between small changes and big changes, and there's a difference between being and seeming. There's arbitrary boundaries, and there's fixed boundaries, and there's boundaries in between. There's the anecdote of the boiling frog, where if you turn up the heat slowly it lets itself get cooked, demonstrating the slippery slope of creeping normality.

Some have attempted to solve the riddle by simply gauging public opinion, creating a survey scale, not unlike the Panic and Agoraphobia Scale that I've been doing for therapy. The choices include: definitely heap, mostly heap, partly heap, slightly heap, and not heap.

Maybe not with grains of sand, but with bodies, I think only one may be sufficient to constitute a heap.

Last night at my hostel, I crunched some numbers to take my mind off things, calculating the cubic volume of humanity. The average person is about seventy liters, so multiply that by our current population estimate of seven billion, and you get 490 billion liters, or lets call it half a trillion liters. One cubic mile holds 4,168,181,825,440 liters, ignoring the fraction, so let's round it to four trillion liters. We see the total human volume is about one-eighth the number of liters in a cubic mile. There are eight half-mile cubes stacked together in one cubic mile, and just one of them would hold every human on the planet. One cube, about 2,600 feet on each side. Of course you would have to put them in a blender or something first to get that kind of raw volume, but still, it's quite the image to consider.

Canetti has a powerful passage in his book about contemplating the greatest density of humans—it's what led me to mull over the math—and when you imagine all those who have ever lived, the box doesn't really get that much bigger. Some anthropologists say the number is only about fourteen times larger. There were so few *Homo sapiens* for so long that they don't really add up to much volume, and even with every human that has ever lived inside it, the box would still be smaller than two cubic miles. If you're having problems visualizing two cubic miles, a huge volcanic mountain like Rainier is around thirty-four cubic miles I think, and if you were to fall through the air for one vertical mile, you would have about twenty seconds before splat. Considering crowds like Canetti did, we can be reasonably sure the largest crowds are the already dead, but it's difficult to know if the future dead will out-number them, to know if they'll be a bigger pile, requiring a significantly larger box.

In sand paintings done by Vajrayana Buddhists, Mount Meru is the ultimate heap, the center of all the universes, and there is some overlap with the mountain called Kailash by the Hindus. Meru is thought of as Shiva's home, and many Hindu, Buddhist, and Jain temples are built to resemble the mythical mountain, usually involving concentric circles. If you blur your vision a little when you're looking at the Buddhist sand paintings of Meru, they can resemble the Mayan calendar, or the Aztec Sun Stone, and Abelian sandpiles too. It makes sense that a mountain would symbolize the home of gods. The largest possible heap is perhaps the best illustrator of gravity, itself one of our biggest gods.

While we're talking about Mount Impossible and human volume, it is an important question whether or not the projected world population increase necessarily correlates to increased stampede fatalities in the future. Will population density play a large role in the body counts to come, or will the numbers depend more on infrastructure and education?

In the past, obtaining accurate crowd size data wasn't easy. It still isn't. Reaching a perspective from which you can simultaneously photograph the entire scene often proves impossible, and getting composite shots from multiple locations to be stitched together usually requires that you know where the crowd will be in advance. Aircraft with telephoto equipment, combined with clear skies, create the most reliable data, but planes are beyond the financial reach of most data quests. The arrival of UAVs is radically improving the accuracy of crowd size estimates—drones are changing everything—but monied interests and politics continue to influence the reportage and

to warp the stats. It doesn't matter what the numbers are if
they're reported incorrectly. "How many people were there?"
has been one of the most important questions of all narratives
forever, so lying about the size of the crowd must be an age-
old practice too.

Crowd crush data exploded in the late twentieth century
along with data for everything else, but inferring backward
suggests true historical casualty numbers might be staggering.
How many humans have died in stampedes throughout all the
eras? We'll never know, but we just might get good numbers
on the future, which means the present wobbles in a dynamic
position.

In his book *Complexity*, Mitchell Waldrop writes about complex adaptive systems anticipating the future, and making
projections based on different models. One problem is
that the predictions aren't always right, and sometimes the
intertwined systems confuse each other. One could say that,
in general, crowd crush is a problem of too many complex systems—otherwise known as humans—functioning together. At
a certain level of interconnectivity you get causal feedback,
then you're fucked.

The Game of Life is another computer program like the
Abelian sandpile, that allows for observation of the way
complex patterns can emerge from the implementation
of very simple rules. In most iterations, the Game of Life
looks like the primitive computer games of the 1970s, and it
involves simple shapes assigned to point values plotting their
own courses across the screen, left to play out their lives

according to a few math rules. Given the right values plugged in, the shapes establish fascinating patterns of behavior. Some transform into more complicated shapes and go into repeating a never-ending loop. Other configurations might smash into each other and end, while still others become immobile behemoths. There are patterns that seem to be everlasting, and others that burn out fast. An infinite number of variables and grid sizes means that anyone playing with the numbers might see a pattern roll across their screen that has never before been witnessed in this universe. Given a handful of rules for actions, a tiny flowchart, a very simple decision tree, and only a few components, life will sometimes hobble together an ongoing complexity out of chaos. It will scramble out of the sandpile and emerge from the rubble like me and my crappy blog. An emergent property is not a property of any component of the system, but is still a feature of the system.

It is said that the emergent quality need not be more complicated than the underlying non-emergent properties that generate it. The magic that shows up doesn't have to be smart magic, it can be just as dumb as its parts. But before the magic shows up, a system must reach a combined threshold of diversity, organization, and connectivity. Does this seem sufficiently diverse, organized, and connected?

Time seems so strange and vital that it must be an emergent property of another system such as gravity. I have read theories suggesting that time moves one way because of a contrast in entropy between what cannot be said to be now, and now, but it seems like the second law of thermodynamics and time are the same thing, saying fuck you to chaos and gravity. And then life comes along and says fuck you to time and entropic principles.

Physicists say the future will be so much more distorted than the now, as everything continues to get stretched out, but that for the most part there is an irreversibility to the whole. It goes one way, it cannot be unstretched, and up is up and down is down when you're forced to stack anything. You really can't accomplish much without stacking things. Even enlightenment, even the abandonment of everything, generally requires some sequence of steps that are stacked. Maybe Shiva can come and go from Mount Meru without effort, but everyone else climbs. Even if you were to say the path leads downhill, there is up/down direction involved. Everything is stacked on top of everything. Psychological properties supervene on the biological properties, then on the chemical, then on the atomic. You might call it downward causation. But property is just another way of saying perspective. You say the bird is blue, but the bird doesn't understand. So then the causation chain is based on perspective. You stand on the mountain, and the mountain is on the earth, and the earth sits on some elephants, and they're standing on a turtle, and the turtle rests on a serpent, and the serpent is swallowing its tail...

But does stacking mean anything in the inverse? I don't mean just undoing the stacking. Unstacking would simply add another related event. I mean a way in which already dissimilar objects continue to become even more unconnected and independent of each other. Akin to the way things get forgotten or left behind, but more like when they've never even been considered. Is there an Angel of Oblivion standing back-to-back with the Angel of History in Walter Benjamin's Klee painting? One that watches, not as things keep piling wreckage upon wreckage, but as things get farther and farther apart and fail to pile upon each other? Who looks on as things become safe, and calm, and untouched, by avoiding having anything to do with one another?

Certainly the Angel of History is there, and the pile of wreckage grows. Just look at the news so far this year, and everything that started with Mohamed Bouazizi, the Tunisian produce vendor who died on January 4th from burns suffered while immolating himself in mid December. Revolts were set off in Tunisia, then Egypt, then they picked up the label "Arab Spring" and kept going. Now Syria is ramping up towards civil war, and the spring seems to have settled into its own state of continual collapse.

In stranger news, for the most part without being told, US taxpayers financed Afghanistan's new TV cop show that's airing its first season. It's called Eagle Four, and it features caricatures of an elite Afghan police unit bringing the dream of stability to the impossibly unstable. Gaddafi was seen on TV this February pleading for help fighting terrorists, un-derlining that for some time now the word terrorism hasn't meant anything. You might as well just say life is terrorism, if someone hasn't already said it. In early March, the Pope finally exonerated the Jews for killing Jesus, and then, about a week later, the Tōhoku earthquake and tsunami wiped every-thing else out of the news for a while.

With a magnitude estimated around 9.1, the tectonic activity

moved Japan's main island Honshu eight feet closer to
California in a matter of minutes. The tsunami that followed
the quake became the single most destructive event ever
caught on camera. Nothing from nuclear bomb detonations
comes even close in resolution and overwhelming detail. I remember being glued to my laptop in the days that followed, as
more and more footage was uploaded. My anxieties exploded.
So many different perspectives of horror. Helicopter footage
of the wave shot near Iwate Prefecture is requisite viewing
for anyone who hasn't seen it, anyone who can handle it.
The remains of an entire urban area float atop the advancing
sea, and in some places, whole massive factories on fire are
levitated, and join the wreckage headed inland. The close-ups
of the wall of water moving across farm fields, eating everything, at over a hundred miles an hour, will give many people
nightmares. You can watch as cars fleeing just ahead of the
wave lose the race.

Other footage demonstrates that a tsunami's process doesn't
always manifest like the iconic wall of water at all, but more
like a massive upswell. Whole bays appear to grow from below
as the water pumps in beneath them, and their regular boundaries—the shores, the levees, the docks—are superseded all
at once, often going through several cycles of in and out,
grinding everything against everything multiple times.

It's impossible to predict what will happen when that much
water gets sloshed around. Sometimes clapotis gets exhib-
ited, when waves moving in different directions intersect at
particular angles and their oscillations magnify each other like
feedback, causing sudden, dramatic surges, seemingly out

of nowhere. In some places around Sendai, the water levels exceeded all the worst case scenario predictions.

At least sixteen thousand deaths are attributed to the earthquake, the tsunami, and their aftermath. The human totals didn't seem to get much play in the States though. Instead of joining the Japanese in a deep mourning, most of the US news media focused on the ongoing crisis at the Fukushima Daiichi nuclear power facilities, and what was effectively sold to viewers as a ticking time bomb situation. Level 7 meltdowns at multiple reactors. A great description of my anxieties lately.

Afterward there was talk about Fukushima's fallout getting added to the list of useful date markers frozen into the ice at the poles, and layered into the globe's soils. The Cesium 137 that fell in 1987 and 1988, and all the others. Strontium 90, iodine 131, plutoniums 239 and 240, americium 241. The scientists that use the data for their calendars describe it as traces of radiation, as if radiation can be said to be anything else besides traces. Isn't spacetime itself just the ephemeral evidence of universal decay?

The Tōhoku event moved our planet's axis at least four inches over, and shortened each of our days on earth by about two millionths of a second. It involved what geophysicists call a nutation. A hiccup in the globe's precession, like when the dance of a spinning top takes a little wobble, then resumes a regular ellipse. It's another great analog for my psychological problems, as in, "I think I'm going to have another nutation."

When I read some of the science about the world wobble, it

was described as following the earthquake, but did the tremor cause the nutation, or was it part of it? Thinking about a spinning top, isn't it easy to imagine that the nutation needed to happen, and that it required some tectonic adjustments to precede it in order to perform its correction? Doesn't it seem like the two events are probably really one larger event? The way an ice skater tucks in an arm or leg, which then changes their center of gravity, and thus the velocity of their spin.

The date of the earthquake, March 11, was the same as Madrid's Atocha bombings seven years earlier, so now two countries are saddened by the same numbers: 11/3. After that, on March 20, some asshole burned a copy of the Koran in Florida, and while nobody got hurt in the US, at least thirty died worldwide in the riots that erupted in its wake. Then the news reported leaks at WikiLeaks, the world reached 800 million vehicles on the roads, Obama created the Department of Misinformation, and multiple international skirmishes erupted because Google was selling maps with different political boundaries to different customers. They assassinated Bin Laden on May 2, but his wives were free to go after the raid, and not charged with aiding a terrorist like they would be in most Western democracies. The US news media played up the last flight of the Space Shuttle on July 21, but in all their hoopla they never mentioned that it was only the end of the *piloted* shuttle, and that we've had the *unmanned* X-37 shuttle going to space and back since April of last year. Supposedly it's a secret, but you've been able to read about it on Wikipedia since before its first launch. The day after that, the monster Breivik killed ninety-two in Norway, maybe a world record, and the dickhead trolls, intensely proud of him, came out in force, excited about a new number for assholes everywhere to overcome. Courts made incursions into the prosecution of future crimes, the CIA aired now-hiring ads on FM radio nationally, and flamingos were reported in Siberia, apparently a problem related to a reversed interpretation of polarity. Riots broke out in England on August 6, and the shit must be in the air, because right now, contemporaneous with my travel, the Occupy movement has been hunkered down in Lower Manhattan for a while, and it doesn't seem to be going anywhere anytime soon.

Which reminds me of me. I stop typing to look around the café setting, but there's nothing of interest happening. I check a weather website, and a pop-up ad forces me to click on the word "collapse" to get rid of it.

So what happens in this post? Does something else have to go down, or is traveling here enough to constitute a happening? Can't I just say I journeyed to India, and everyone else will do the work of conjuring up the exotic and the extraordinary? The Taj Mahal will flash through their minds, and they will see tiger hunts and elephants. It happens whether or not I write about it, so why do anything? We're nine posts into nowhere. I would have liked to produce a good blog, but the time is past in which I could improve it. Some famous author said literature is crap. I don't remember which, but there must have been others.

Nothing but disjointed drafts. Nothing but a poioumenon, a tabulation of nonsense, the semblance of a weblog. Piles of ghosts. The ghosts of things that could have happened, in a heap, neither present or absent, demonstrating that being does not have to involve reality.

Is there another version where I'm laying over in Delhi instead of Mumbai? Did my flight come in above the nested circles and triangles of the capital city's downtown area and not the Arabian Sea? Is there another version where I'm just making it all up, copying shit off the internet in Seattle? I've read some Joyce, I don't have to be in Dublin, and I can just shove anything I want into the works, can't I?

Is the blog more realistic if I'm taking care of my needs, like sleep, and pissing, and meds? Or does it make a better read if I ignore these and have something of a motivation? Should reality be the subject, or is it okay to slip into more like a fictional non-fiction?

I'll play out this post just sitting here. This will be a work haunted by what hasn't happened. But something not happening is not the same thing as nothing happening. Something not happening requires that it could have happened, while nothingness has no stipulations.

Perhaps it's the mountain of ghosts of what cannot happen, of the impossible, that might be the most terrifying heap.

I will continue to avoid doing anything besides getting my work done. I will not be at greater risks than back home. Nothing I see in India will resemble a crowd crush event. Of course, anyone who wants more data on stampedes inevitably considers how easy it would be to start one himself. There are solid reasons why it's a crime to scream "Fire!" in a crowded

theater. The idea highlights the difference between misinformation and disinformation, and demonstrates they might
produce the exact same results despite different motives.

I have imagined constructing a crush-proof vest, similar to the
plastic turtle shells they already have for severe osteoporosis
patients, and I have imagined testing it. I have envisioned
it both working and failing. Dying in a crowd collapse event
already seems more self-inflicted than other disasters, like the
species turning against itself. Dying in one you start yourself
would be well deserved, and doubly suicidal.

Survivors often mention the similarity between crowd crush
and drowning. It boils down to the inability to breathe.
Drowning in people. But when crowd crush survivors say it
feels like drowning, how do they know what it feels like unless
they've already drowned? I've said similar things about my
anxieties but I've never drowned. Do we just instinctively
know what it feels like? Is it as simple as holding your breath?

At 54,000 people per square mile, Mumbai is comparable
to Paris. I'm trying to look at the sameness, not the difference, and to have faith in my decisions as I head back into the
streets, but each tiny left or right overwhelms. All the ones
and zeros of Zoroaster's good and bad. Didn't the Indians
invent zero, or was it the Persians? You would think that all
zeros are the same nothing, but mathematicians know well
that there are different kinds of zeros.

If projections are correct, India will be the world's most
populous nation by 2028, and it's hard not to feel the upswell

testing the seams. The noise level suggests the volume keeps getting pushed up.

But maybe I'm all wrong about what the future will look like here. Maybe science will eventually bring a world without crowds, where either necessity or convenience ends with everyone staying in their own little bubble.

There's danger in tight coupling, you're better off alone. What the science has already shown for sure is that you're more likely to survive catastrophes without dependents or partners.

It's probably a good thing that I'm by myself.

Writing the blog has turned out to be a very useful tool for shutting out the world. Who was it that said write like you're dead?

Sending.

JODHPUR

October 10, 2011

2008 Jodhpur Stampede   blog lit

Chamunda Devi   denouement

haveli   hello/goodbye

Mehrangarh Fort   pratītyasamutpāda

Toorji's Stepwell   unknots

Welcome to my blog, it's over. Hello and goodbye. Everything is fucked, and nothing is fucked. I'll just leave this here on top of the stack. On the homepage right now, this one's the first one you see, but it's really underneath all the others. Nothing is stopping the reader from opening all the posts at once and displaying the entire sequence simultaneously in ten overlapping windows. Nothing protects its chronology.

Total dumbass that I am, I lost my bag and missed my meetings. Much of this blogpost was initially written on paper. Eventually my bag was returned to me with all its contents intact.

I'm ready to be done with this. I don't think I need it anymore. I wouldn't say I'm feeling better, but I'm over the hump, and will be home soon. I crunched my PAS numbers and there's no change, even after the vision I had.

The impulse to run away and hide in a hole has been strong, but nothing unusual. I am writing instead of running again, and the undertaking often looks like I'm not doing anything at all. I have imagined filming an instructional video for YouTube entitled "How to Write a Blog," including painfully long sequences of me sitting at a table doing nothing. Sometimes I play with my pen.

After I checked my PAS score, I looked at my blog stats. The bar graphs that represent its popularity don't show any up or down, and my hits per hour/day/week/month are unchanged. Every time I'm at the control panel I wrestle with whether or not to enable the comments button and open the blog up to opinions, but I end up reminding myself that this chronicling is supposed to be a therapy tool, not an invitation for others to further undermine my psyche.

It looks like someone in Albania has visited a few times recently, but that's about it. With hundreds of millions of blogs, why would anyone look at mine? Because people go into random caves to hide? I imagine my blog as part of the electric hive's strange, dark geology, resembling the digital, three-dimensional maps of limestone cave systems. It is compartmentalized anti-space, sometimes providing a place to hole up.

Somebody said that these days you've got to self-curate or you disappear, but then you're forced into decisions about what to include or discard in your part of the hive. Obama said something recently about "choosing our better history," and I can't help but make another comparison to lossy data. Reality gets compressed, and redundant or shitty info gets deleted for more efficient storage. To create the simulacrum, much of it gets left out.

I prefer to disappear anyway. Well, maybe I should say I'm inclined to. Even the simplest organisms aren't much more than code transfer devices. Unless I have offspring, my genetic info won't get uploaded again, and at most I will have been used by parasites to pass on their DNA sequences, but not my own. Perhaps I'm wrong, but I've never heard of a famous blogger. Blogging is like the opposite of literature. Somebody said literature should be written by non-literary people. Because they're without a central conflict, and they pile up any which way, blogs signal the end of story. But stories were always imaginary anyway, right? Consequences don't necessarily exist outside of human thought.

Now the screens are designed to make you link to another site, not to move on to the next page in a specified sequence. Is reading my blog posts ten-through-one, instead of one-through-ten, like seeing the future only to find the anachronistic information useless? If I kept going, and you perused them backward, you could quite possibly arrive here already having seen what I cannot now know. But instead of making for a better read it fucks it all up. Like in that movie *Memento*, except it just gets more confusing instead of less. Beginning, middle, and end come at random, like a *Choose Your Own Adventure* book that doesn't work. *Hopscotch* while having a panic attack.

Somebody said that most tourists visit places for something that isn't really there, and it's probably true about travel blogs too. Is that something that isn't there the same as that mythic something more we hear of?

I am writing to buffer both sides of the impossibilities.

There was the 5 a.m. call to prayer in Mumbai, but between the jet lag and the meds time seemed relative. In movies, the muezzin singing at dawn provides the soundtrack for the classic framing shot, but it had no cinematic effect on me. It didn't place or organize my point of view, my sense of continuity. At best it complicated the cacophony.

There was a taxi to Dadar Terminus, and inside the station a grand arched hall similar to Gare du Nord in Paris, but minus the frills. The scene was more *Slumdog Millionaire* now, and I tried to ignore most of it so I could keep my shit together. It wasn't rush hour, but the crowds were still substantial, and watching the train screech to a stop I thought about the early Lumiere film of a locomotive arriving in its station. His late nineteenth century Parisian audience stampeded inside the theater as the steam engine got closer and closer. They didn't understand the projected illusion, and many of the patrons preferred not being run over by the image to testing for themselves its insubstantiality. While the engine at the head of my train was yellow and purple, the carriage was to be dark blue, with a teal stripe where the windows ran.

The Western Railways logo involves a red circle with a white center, inside of which an antique locomotive barrels at the observer from the left. An upside down swoosh of smoke coming from the top of the engine suggests speed. Seventeen gold stars circle the central image, and its white background is sliced up by nine horizontal bands. What's known as the Lion Capital of Ashoka, the image of four lions sitting back-to-back on a wheel, ornaments the face of the oncoming train.

I was taking an overnight second-class sleeper, and my compartment had six bunks, just like on the trip to Asturias from Barcelona. It was disconcerting the way the windows had thick bars over them so you couldn't use them to get in or out. For certain the sealed windows cause higher fatalities when there are wrecks, fires, attacks, and bombings. They're pretty much the opposite of emergency exits. I already knew Indian trains were like this, but now I was actually inside the situation. An Indian might reply that every year legal guns in the United States kill tens of thousands more people than bars on Indian train windows do. Another great example of cultural differences in freedom/safety compromises.

The decor was gray formica with a mild herringbone pattern and blue seats, blue trim. A family from Gujarat was to share the compartment with me and they were very friendly. There was a pantry car, but it wasn't necessary because vendors came by every few minutes with tea, coffee, water, samosas, vadas, and newspapers.

We stopped in Borivali, then Vapi, and at some point I heard loud hand claps before a small group of what looked like men dressed as women entered our compartment and stood around the entrance. There was a short exchange between the father from Gujarat and our visitors, and they were obviously talking about me at one point. Some rupees were given to them, they departed, and then the gentleman from Gujarat looked at me and said, "Eunuchs," which made little sense until I was able to look up Indian transgender culture online later.

We came to Surat, and then around Vadodara Junction my neighbors unpacked from vessels inside vessels an insane amount of food, and had a family feast. Numerous times they encouraged me to join them, but I was worried about my stomach. I was already thinking about this blog post, and about quitting it, and about the lost in-betweens and for-forgotten beloveds that wouldn't make it in if I stopped.

I wanted to say something about Chongqing in 1941, when the Japanese bombing caused a crowd crush event in which more than four thousand people died. It was perhaps the worst crowd event ever recorded, but it is difficult to separate the deaths caused by the bombs from the deaths caused by asphyxiation. And I wanted to mention the shitshow that was Stalin's funeral in 1953, where even horses were reported to have been pulled down and smothered. And the poorly reported and little understood Luzhniki disaster, Moscow 1982, with no accurate body count, or the well known Hillsborough soccer match in 1989 that left ninety-six dead and which is still under litigation today, an obvious coverup.

Just two years ago, there were several casualties here in India during the exceptionally long solar eclipse, which brought millions to the sacred places along the banks of the Ganges near Varanasi, and earlier this year, there was a stampede during

the annual pilgrimage to Sabarimala that left one hundred
and six dead. The Sabarimala event remains very mysterious
because it happened in an open field, free from any of the
obstructions and landscape features that generally accompany
high fatalities. I thought about it as a possible study subject,
but it seemed to lack any measurable data.

We came to Anand Junction, then Nadiad Junction around
nightfall. Trying to sleep on the train, with the clickety-clack
an almost constant, I reclined on the edge of a waking dream
about all the things that would be left out.

What does it say that *Escape* is at the top left on the key-
board, almost exactly opposite of *Enter*? And the other keys
that say things—*Shift*, *Alternate*, *Control*—all of them seem to
work with my subject too. And what about the images? A tiny
magnifying glass, a tiny lock, a tiny speaker, a tiny gear, a tiny
sun, little boxes inside each other, an arrow going in a circle.
Home is a button on a billion keyboards. *Hide* is a top row
function, and you toggle to the operation above, not below.
There is no opposite of superposition. No easy way to say
that two things are becoming less connected. You can't just
slip things in underneath the stack. Bottlenecks in irreduc-
ibly complex systems, dead ends, irregular pathway choices,
pressure points—all of them apply to both crowd science and
my attempts to write down my life. Social networking equals
entanglement, equals tragedy of the common denominator.
Progressively prosthetic relations, distributed cognition, colony collapse disorder, open source culture, boundary control,
terror tourism, code switching, trending subvertisements,
adhocracy, peak everything, digital deicide.

The station stops during the night are quiet, and it's hard to see anything outside but their illuminated names: Ahmedabad Junction, Mahesana Junction. Shadows come and go in the hallway.

More thoughts about flock as organism, communal brain, shared mind, oversoul, and all the other words for crowd. Attendance, assemblage, audience, multitude, set, lot, congregation. And the assembly turns its collective attention toward machines. The crowdsourcing narcisystem functions on the asynchronous viewing of our multiscreen reality, a universe more palimpsestuous than holographic. Clickstream behavior, locational awareness, locative media, medialess products, transmedia, accelerated media environment. TBIs and ELEs, fusion centers, communication management units, and digital rights discussions.

Palanpur Junction.

A delusional parasitosis spreads to computer operating systems, and its opposite, a silicon satori, brings with it e-everything, and post-PC nothingness. Thuggish time brings along link rot, and avatar fatigue, and Gilliamesques, and embolisms, and everything that is not yet, what has yet to come to be, the heretical-by-nature future. A solid state salmagundi with its optimization algorithms proving all the no-free-lunch theorems. Chaos machines and strange attractors, traumatologists with their counter-misinformation, phase transitions moving along discrete packages, cerebral fistulas growing into unexpected passages. Asymmetrical aggregation of apotropaic analogues resulting in phthalate mutations, plastic gods off-gassing endocrine disruptors.

In the morning we passed through Bhildi Junction, Dhanera, Raniwara. The journey had started out green, but now the landscape was desert-like. Heading almost directly north from Mumbai, just about a thousand kilometers, we were rolling through the world of dust devils and arid thorn scrub. Out the window I spotted gray langur monkeys for the first time, and saw an old man managing angry looking camels. If you watch *The Darjeeling Limited* you might get the idea. Sometimes it looked like the same scenery was getting repeated, just going by the window in the opposite order.

Marwar Bhinmal, Modran, then we arrived in Jodhpur. The number of stops was the same as it was in Atlanta on the MARTA train. I felt like I might have an episode, but the clamor died down.

Anyone asked to describe Jodhpur must start by saying that it's blue, and I'm no exception. It's blue. It's a weird thing for a city to be blue. It reminds me of that old Paul Mauriat song "Love is Blue." My dad used to play it on vinyl. To be fair, not every building in Jodhpur is painted blue, but there's enough to make it stand out as predominant—maybe 20 percent of them in certain districts—and much of the municipal infrastructure matches as well.

I'm in the state of Rajasthan now, and this area is part of the ancient Wool Route that fed into the so-called Silk Road, something that really needs to be visualized as an agglomerated network, instead of a line with one product. The Vaishnava sect predominates in the region, and apparently many wealthy Jains play dominant roles in the social structure locally.

The room I reserved was in a haveli, a type of old mansion that is frequently converted into a kind of boarding house, or small hotel. As with most havelis, a large courtyard presided at the center of the edifice, and balconies and verandas were incorporated on all sides of it. Mrs. Dita Joshi and her family lived in rooms blocked off to the public on the northwest side of the building. She met me at the door, checked me in, and gave me a brief tour of the amenities. It was nice to have a private space again, but I was surprised that I still felt like leaving and exploring after I was shut inside.

Following a brief reset, I mustered up my courage and went out to explore the neighborhood, and very shortly I stumbled upon the stepwell. I didn't know what one was, and when I saw the sign, "Stepwell Café," I liked the name. I imagined it had to do with good choices along one's path, but then I heard the sounds of screaming children playing, and I caught a faint whiff of moisture. I turned a corner and there was a large opening between the buildings, and as I got closer I could see there was nothing there. What I mean to say is that there was a huge emptiness, a massive excavation, a humongous hole. Concentric stone terraces with multiple mirrored staircases dropped down into each other, getting smaller and smaller, until they reached the rippled surface of their precious purpose, a cool pool of green-blue water in which children were swimming and splashing.

The stepwell in Jodhpur is one of the most beautiful things I have ever seen. The arrangement of staircases forms a reducing

criss-cross pattern like an inclined maze, the opposite of a
ziggurat, right out of an Escher print, and the effect of standing
on its rim is simultaneously vertiginous and ecstatic. One side
is devoted to a massive arched recess, and I imagine it housed
the statue of a deity in former times. Its eminence would have
emerged slowly from the well's waters as they were used up
by the community during the dry months, and during the wet
season, the god would have slowly disappeared beneath the
water again, as the reservoir filled up to capacity. Without a
god in the recess, the hollow frames a divine vacuum. I sat for a
while on the well's edge and marveled at both its simplicity and
its complexity, at how nothingness is required to put something
somewhere, an ornamented hole that allows gravity to nestle
our most important commodity together.

It's called Toorji's Stepwell, and the Stepwell Café sits right
above it. The sounds of the kids playing are coming in through
the windows right now while I write this. People who have
visited the 9/11 Memorial's twin holes in Manhattan can appreciate the way approaching an emptiness, with the horizon
continuing to drop away, elicits a powerful feeling. The reverse
of monument might be a summary of monument. While the
architecture in Manhattan holds you back from seeing the
bottom, here in Jodhpur you're welcome to go over the rim.
Supposedly security guards come around a few times a day
and scare the children off, but I have yet to see anyone disturbing them, and some of the teenagers make daring jumps
from the higher terraces. I tried to imagine jumping in.

This morning, Dita offered me kachori and pao at breakfast.
With so many things I could describe, the travel blog becomes

a game about what to leave out more than what to put in. Do I talk about dal, and chapatis, and guavas? Tridents and tuning fork on foreheads? Groups of children playing cricket, broken glass bangles underfoot everywhere, homespun dhotis, and beedi butts with their tiny strings? Harijan and hanuman-jis, yakshis and marigolds, incense sticks, drums, kumkum, chickpea salesmen, ice cream wallahs, bullock carts, kids flying kites, men wearing white and saffron turbans, women in blue, or red and green checks, or yellow, or mustard, heavy gold nose rings, silver anklets, peacocks, the janeu threads worn over men's shoulders, boys rolling hoops with sticks, or Dita's calming poise? I give up.

A small group of monkeys has been hanging out on a rooftop nearby, and several of them have come down onto the ground where I can make out their faces. I can't help but see myself. Maybe I'm glad that writing about what's exotic isn't cool any-more, it lets me focus on my thoughts. Is it completely fucked up to sound more interested in the monkeys than the people? The subject is problematic.

Anyway, backspace a bit. Before it's over, I have to give some summary about the stampede that happened here in Jodhpur a few years ago, in 2008.

On September 30 of that year, around 25,000 devotees had gathered at the fifteenth century temple devoted to Chamunda Devi for the first day of the nine-day Navratri fes-tival. Some reports say that the temple gates were opened at 3:45 a.m., and that everything went fine for about two hours.

The men's queue snaked up a steep, narrow, mile-long path through the passageways that lead to the Mehrangarh Fort, and to the temple on its southwest corner, and the push of the crowd got worse as sunrise approached and the most auspicious time for offering prayers was about to begin. Around 5:30am, a bamboo barricade near the temple gave way, and people stumbled. It is probable that the pressure drop caused by the broken barricade misled the crowd into moving in the worst possible direction, right onto the fallen. It appears that once people began getting crushed in the zone near the barricade, a general panic erupted, with many trying unsuccessfully to reverse their course. There were no dedicated egress routes.

While most incidents of precedence point to the broken barricade as the likely cause, other important factors at the Mehrangarh Fort include the perceived threat of a terrorist bombing, a power outage, and the grounds near the temple being slick with coconut water from hundreds of coconuts cut open as offerings to the goddess. In the months before the festival in Jodhpur, tensions between Muslims and Hindus had led to a series of bombings at busy markets in New Delhi, Malegaon, and Modasa, so the devotees gathered here were understandably on edge. As panic spread, some people were reported yelling about a bomb, and of course this amplified the disaster. Afterward, one of the rescuers said that the bodies had "lay braided together," and that they, "could not pull them out, it was as if they were joined together." Investigations and court cases are ongoing.

It was the fourth fatal temple stampede in India that year. Around 224 died, and more than 400 were injured. Exact numbers are impossible because many families took their dead and injured away without talking to the so-called authorities.

Aftermath has been a thematic word for my studies, and the tally of the dead and the exploration of their statistics has been much of my work. Sometimes my thoughts mull over gravity as the true culprit of it all. Isn't the pile of bodies gravity's fault? Would any of this happen without gravity? Thank you gravity. Fuck you gravity.

I wonder about the gravity of nothing, and what the opposite of gravity would be like. And what's the opposite of entanglement? The opposite of the uncanny? Das unheimliches? Canny?

And I wonder how to write about stampedes without simply engendering more fear. Can it be done in a way that helps, not harms? Can a horror film be educational and terrifying at once? Considering how many millions participate in pilgrimages every year in India and elsewhere without incident, one might actually find it remarkable how safe they are. Despite the dangers, crowds are very safe statistically. I can try to be reassuring.

After the stepwell yesterday afternoon, I continued on to see the Mehrangarh Fort, which looms formidably over this part of the city, and I got most of the way there before realizing that while I was still wearing my small backpack, I did not have my satchel containing everything important.

What followed was an unclear amount of panicked time,

---

without my passport, my laptop, or my medications, running around back and forth like Hagar, looking for my bag, between the haveli and the stepwell, and the road to the fort. I eventually retreated into an unused arcade and tried to disappear while I despaired.

It wasn't long before a guy wearing bluejeans and a Nirvana T-shirt came up and asked me if I was okay. He said he was simply making sure I didn't need anything, and that he didn't want to bother me at all. I said I'm cool, although it was obvious I wasn't, and explained that I had lost my bag.

"I had a feeling there was some trouble," he said.

His name was Rishi, and he was from Jaipur, but he had gone to school in Boston at some point. After hearing of my plight, he said, "Come, come. Consider yourself one of us, dude. You just need a pal for a little while." He offered to accompany me up to the fort if I hadn't seen it yet.

"This is the definition of 'out of your hands' my friend, and what you do about it now matters not in the least. The bag will make it back to you or it won't, but in accordance with other people's actions, not yours."

I said I was going to be fine, but he asked more than once, and he eventually got me to exit the alcove and walk with him. He pointed to a shop ahead of us and said, "But first, would you like to chill out with some nourishment? I know these guys that make baller milkshakes. My treat!"

So we had some milkshakes, and it *did* make me feel better to talk to somebody, and to have something in my stomach. He said he had visited the Mehrangarh Fort with many friends and family in the past, and that he would enjoy being my informal tour guide. He told me that Christian Bale, and a film crew from the next Batman movie, were in town recently, shooting scenes with the fort in the background.

As we made our way uphill, he told me about the legend of Cheeria Nathji, the Lord of Birds, the hermit occupant of the cliffs before the fort was built 600 years ago, who cursed it to be forever dry, and of Raja Ram Meghaval, who, without reluctance, let himself be buried alive in the fort's foundation as a sacrifice.

If you look at the fort using the satellite view like I'm doing, the picture may be confusing because you see large shadows cast by the ridge and the fort toward the northwest. At first they might be mistaken for lakes or reservoirs. Perhaps by the time you read this, the shadows will be gone, and Google will have patched together an impossibly clear view of it all. You can just make out the white-capped gazebo type of thing, overlooking all of Jodhpur at the southwest corner of the fort complex. This is the Temple of Chamunda Devi, the focal point of the 2008 disaster.

Chamunda Devi is one of the Seven Mothers, or matri-kas, and one of the eighty-one yoginis attendant to Durga. Sometimes she is known as Kali, and she is associated with Parvati, and Chandi, and with the Pleiades. She is black, or red, or orangish in color, and she is often depicted wearing a

---

garland of severed heads or skulls. She may carry a *damaru*, a *trishula*, a sword, and *panapatra*, and sometimes she rides a jackal, while other times she is shown standing on the corpse of a man. She often has three eyes, usually a terrifying face and a sunken belly, and her dress is generally of tiger, or lion, or leopard skin. She is said to haunt the places of cremation, and cemeteries, and charnel grounds. She is called Chamunda because she killed the two demons Chanda and Munda.

I asked Rishi about the goddess, and he said that many Westerners confuse the demon named Kali with the goddess named Kali, and he got into talking about the Kali Yuga, the last age before the end of the world, the epoch of disintegration when Vishnu and Shiva are asleep, and the highest deity is seated on a throne constructed of five corpses. I think this is what the taxi driver in Mumbai was bitching about.

He said, "The *error* is that the *era* is named after the demon, not the goddess," and he appeared self-satisfied with his play on words. We were getting higher, and the views were widening out, and he stopped us at a place along a low wall where we could see into the distance.

"It's all a big game of dice, and we rolled the lowest possible throw, meaning the game is done, Krishna has departed, and time will soon stop for just a moment right at the end, before everything starts again. But the way my lord wants things to be, that is the way they are, and death is nothing, only a change of circumstance. If Chamunda Devi decides to destroy you, you are destroyed. Then you must prepare yourself to be destroyed again."

He took in a long breath while gazing out over the plane, and he turned to me and smiled and said, "But I don't actually believe any of that shit. That's just the stuff Brits and Americans love for us to say. I come up here for the views, and the fresh air, and some exercise, not for the temple."

I laughed with him and admitted that I fell for it.

"But it is interesting to note that the stampede you are studying happened in the men's queue, not the women's. And that there appear to be differences between the male gods and the female. It is just like with the Catholics and their Mary. No matter how much the priests try to institute a male god, when people are in trouble they call for their mother, not their father, and she killed many more sons than daughters here."

Rishi looked at the people up ahead and said it might get crowded at the top, and that it might be difficult to make it all the way to the temple today. I asked him if there is a statue or a representation of Chamunda Devi in the temple and he said, "The goddess in the shrine here, she is only a cute little doll, all wrapped up in flowers, with an orange face that is really just two big eyes smiling out at you from the marigolds."

A doll. Didn't someone say gods are just imaginary friends for adults?

The idea of crowds at the top turned my stomach a little.

Rishi looped back to his earlier topic. "But just because I don't believe in a soul, and devils, and an afterlife, doesn't mean that

I dismiss the sound ontological principles of pratītyasamutpāda, of dependent origination and the like."

He said good and evil are relative, but nothing can be performed in isolation, so it makes sense to give some fore-
thought to your actions.

"*Jab yeh hai, woh hai.* When this is, that is. That shit is solid."

He said he gets it though. He understands why people pray at
the temple.

"Whether a god is actually listening or not, there may be a
value in stating what you want and need, or worry about, or in
admitting your sins or your goals in a mindful way. In order to
talk about those things, you have to think about those things,
and thinking is smarter than just always doing whatever the
fuck your balls or your belly tell you to do.

"But all that bullshit about Oppenheimer quoting from the
Bhagavad Ghita about nukes, 'Bursting of a thousand suns,
splendor of the mighty one, I am become death, the shatterer
of worlds,' blah, blah, blah. So it means that Americans learn
about the Gita in association with nuclear weapons, and with
Oppenheimer all worried about what he had done, yaddah,
yaddah, yaddah. As if one little bomb in any way comes even
close to equalling a supreme everything.

"Western science came along in the nineteenth and twentieth centuries and said, wow, these ideas from ancient
Eastern mysticism fit well with our new discoveries, instead of

admitting that the Indian wise men were actually true scientists, long before the word science existed. It's robbery of
intellectual property to say the very least.

"And the circular life stuff, I get that too. Total annihilation
sounds pretty bad until you are told it will happen over and
over again. Finding a correlated pattern in the game helps
make it all seem okay. I get it."

I was feeling the premonitory signals.

The train is coming.

People should have been looking for the safest exits.

I tried to say something to Rishi in acknowledgment of his
thoughts, but I couldn't find the right tense.

Rishi saw me struggling and said, "Whereof someone cannot
speak, thereof a person must be silent," then continued looking out over the blue city.

The last thing I remember him saying was, "Man those were
some good fucking milkshakes."

She was a three-eyed somebody standing on the corpse of a
man. A shining being, and five other radiant somethings, with
the sky as stone, then crystal, then metal, and then a living
star, a sunburst. I felt distributed in space and time. Space
swarmed in my eyes, and time rang in my ears. She stood on
top of me, and she stood on top of a lotus flower, handheld

electronics in her six, eight, ten, twelve, one million arms, one
million media mudras, a jackal, an owl, a demon buffalo with
a bell around its neck, solar orbs disappearing into clouds, the
crone blood-drinking, mouth agape with a tongue of fire, her
protruding teeth dripping red, revolving asuras. She opens
wide and demonstrates the existence of dark matter, the opposite of the entire universe inside her mouth. She turns into
three devils, but the three devils are just one, and the devil
is an angel upside down. She is made of flames. Burning the
witch is throwing the rabbit into the briar patch. The serpent
isn't eating its tail, it's vomiting itself up. The whole thing is a
digestive malfunction, an abortion. Not a symbol of infinity
but of the upset cycle of rejection. A glitched vision, missing
bytes of code, forgotten bits, constantly reformatting, a broken screensaver, the cipher of my destiny erased.

That point where the journey begins is really at the end. I was
here and there, and I am in the future, on the airplane back
to Seattle. In the absence of any kind of love, thinking about
God takes its place. It all flashes back and forth between different outcomes, but never stays on one. I am a crush victim,
or everything is fine, or I'm not even here, I'm at home on the
internet. Or I'm just a character in a novel. With a nonzero
probability, all previous configurations corrupt each other
again, Sisyphus is happy, welcoming back Sirius, and the spi-
der, and the scarab. It's a reversed hourglass, and the demon
dwarf whispers, "You will repeat all of it. Nothing different.
Love it." The seizure augments the actual better than the real.
If you can augur forward, backward is easy. It's an epiphany
of pronouns, a nutation, a pebble in my shoe, and God has no
scruples. There's I and us, and then there's the mob, where I

and us is one. There's the nonce who stands up to the infinite, and thou art that. Hive, pack, womb, the feeling of being surrounded by people, by the crowd, reversed, consoling instead of disturbing. The choices given are reduced to fight or flight, but there is often a third option. Stay still. Be comforted. Working through stages of annihilation, my days were/are/will be numbered, and in the end all I've got is an atom's weight of good or an atom's weight of evil. Maybe there is no cause and effect. Maybe the incoherence of the incoherence proves something, a cryptogram of the everything. Was this to be my undoing, or had terror simply opened the doors of perception? More phobias came forward, obliviphobia, foramiphobia, fears of surveillance, of authentication, of memory loops, singularities. Fear of it all just being a reverse Bildungsroman. Not that that's not a solid plot choice these days. One thing that's sure to come up again is endless return itself. You could say it's in its nature. But the wheel doesn't exist. It's a lie. Let go of it. Infinite spokes surround the hub, but the thing doesn't work without the hole. It's not about the wheel, but the hole. The wheel is nothing without its empty place.

I came to my senses with my head against a wall looking at the ground, scared to turn around. Rishi was gone and I never ran into him again. I don't blame him for splitting—the drowning often drown their rescuers.

A postictal euphoria swept over me. A few people stared at me strange as they passed, but I tried to laugh it off.

And that's all. Call it an attack, a vision, a breakdown, whatever. With a panic attack there's no so-called story, though to the sufferer, it might be the ultimate incursion of the unreal into the real.

I walked back down the hill from the fort, and now you can scroll back down to the present café setting, with the screams and watery echoes of the stepwell coming in through the windows.

During my episode, I thought she was holding a noose, and I saw online that some depictions of Shakti include one, but as I looked into it, I learned that a noose may be many different iterations of various slipknots used to cinch loads. What is called a hangman's knot is the one many westerners will picture when they hear the word noose, but it appears to be a relatively recent contrivance. Looking into what exactly constitutes a noose was to open up an entirely different pathway.

On the Wikipedia page for knots, there is a great animation of what's called an *unknot* unknotting. A mass of tangled, twisted rope, which looks impossibly bound up, starts to undo itself, one end uncurling and disentwining from the rest, but never having to pass through itself, until at the end there is no knot. It disappears as if by magic because it never really was a knot in the first place. I found the web page and its connected pages fascinating. What constitutes a knot is strictly defined by math and physics, and if the thread doesn't loop back within itself, or around itself, it doesn't count.

The unknotting animation is so amazing that I'm tempted to insert a hyperlink in the blog, but I don't want to go down that rabbithole, or the whole damn document would become opportunities to leave it. Opening those floodgates would turn the chronicle into a deluge of departures, and when the entire thing is hyperlinked, nothing is hyper anymore.

Like with human knots following a crowd crush event, most will fail when trying to describe the unknot. There's got to be some hitch, or splice, or something, but in the end there's nothing holding it all together.

The physical science of knots generally considers twists, friction, and complexity in relation to strength, while some of the math and topography of knots verges on the metaphysical. For us Westerners, Alexandre-Théophile Vandermonde gave knots a mathematical base, and then Dowker and Thistlethwaite came up with a way to map them. What's known as the Dowker-Thistlethwaite notation technique counts positive and negative traversals starting at a random place, and a knot reconstruction based on its coding might end with a mirror of the original knot, as the system doesn't account for chirality.

There's *The Ashley Book of Knots*, there are "prime" knots, and you can read about the difference between knots and links, which just might lead you to consider the similarities between unknots and holes. There's Solomon's knot, and there's Indra's knot, and the endless/eternal knot of Tibetan Buddhism, sometimes referred to as a 7_4 knot, where emptiness is linked to interdependent causation.

People often say things unravel, but ravel is a word too.

Then there's those other kinds of knots, like in psychology, or like the tragic knot of literature and the performing arts, the one the protagonist must free, or untie, or resolve, unless, like Alexander of Macedonia facing the impossible Gordian knot, he simply cuts it in half with his sword.

Looking into the Gordian knot might lead you to click on Star Trek's Kobayashi Maru scenario, in which Starfleet cadets are tested in no-win simulations. A great life metaphor. All of us born into unwinnable situations.

And as for a denouement—French for unknotting, from the Latin *nodus*—there is none, because there was never a knot to untie. The plot is neither a U-shape, nor an inverted U-shape. The trajectory remains an uncertainty, and might depend on what link brought you to which of my posts. This post won't sum up anything, or bring together all the loose ends, or untie them. You can't undo nothing.

It's like the solution to the old bent nail puzzle, with the two linked nails, twisted around each other in unclosed loops. Suddenly, when fidgeted a certain way, there is no more linkage, and they come apart, one in each hand, and indeed it seems subsequently that they could never have been linked to begin with.

In the aftermath, zero.

Sending.

Carlos José Camblor was born in the suburbs of Atlanta, Georgia and holds degrees in Literature from the University of Colorado, Boulder (BA 1992) and the University of Georgia, Athens (MA 2019). For many years he has called Orcas Island, Washington his home.

9 780578 364124